GAELEN FOLEY

One Moonlit Night

MOONLIGHT SQUARE: A PREQUEL NOVELLA

Also By Gaelen Foley

Ascension Trilogy
The Pirate Prince
Princess
Prince Charming

Knight Miscellany
The Duke
Lord of Fire
Lord of Ice
Lady of Desire
Devil Takes a Bride
One Night of Sin
His Wicked Kiss

The Spice Trilogy
Her Only Desire
Her Secret Fantasy
Her Every Pleasure

The Inferno Club
My Wicked Marquess
My Dangerous Duke
My Irresistible Earl
My Ruthless Prince
My Scandalous Viscount
My Notorious Gentleman
Secrets of a Scoundrel

Age of Heroes
Paladin's Prize

**Gryphon Chronicles
(Writing as E.G. Foley)**
The Lost Heir
Jake & the Giant
The Dark Portal
The Gingerbread Wars
Rise of Allies

**50 States of Fear
(Writing as E.G. Foley)**
*The Haunted Plantation
(Alabama)*
*Leader of the Pack
(Colorado)*
*Bringing Home Bigfoot
(Arkansas)*
*Dork and the Deathray
(Alaska)*

Anthologies
Royal Weddings
Royal Bridesmaids

Credits and Copyright

Table of Contents

About the Author

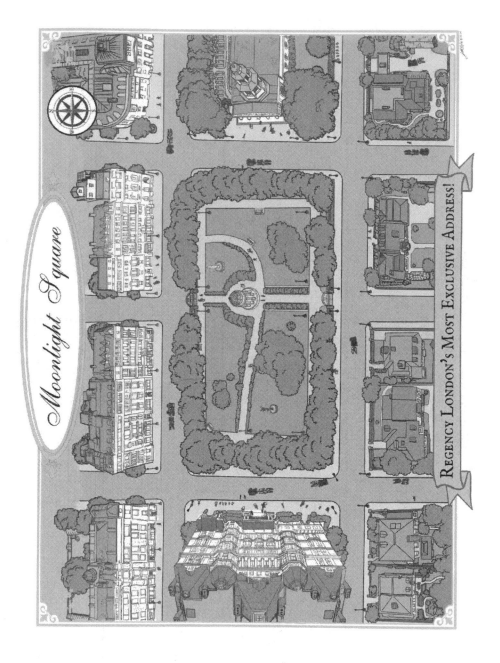

Moonlight Square

Regency London's Most Exclusive Address!

CHAPTER 1

Star-Crossed

*I*t was battle royal in the Beresford household, and eldest daughter Lady Katrina Glendon felt herself under attack from all sides.

All five of her younger sisters were hollering at her at once, some in tears, others wailing that they'd all end up spinsters because of her.

"Papa, she's ruining my life!"

"Mine too!"

"*And* she wrecked my favorite hat!" Lady Betsy screeched, while the youngest, Lady Jane, aged thirteen, kicked the wall because nobody ever listened to her.

The purest rage, however, came from Lady Abigail, sister number two, aged twenty: the prettiest. "How long do you expect Freddie to wait for me, Trinny?" she demanded, taking an angry step toward her. "If I lose him just because you're too much of an odd duck to land a husband—"

"Now, Abby, that is taking it much too far," Papa interjected, appearing in the drawing room doorway with a vexed frown when the volume of the noise had overcome even his will to ignore his chaotic household. "Your sister is not an odd *duck*."

"Oh, yes, she is Papa!" Abby ground out. "That's why none of her suitors ever asked to marry her! You have to *do* something about her before Freddie gives up on me! Are we supposed to wait forever before we can marry?"

"He's not going to give up on you, Abby. That boy would walk through fire for you," Trinny answered, head down, her breath nearly

One Moonlit Night　　1

stolen by the pain of her sister's cruel-but-true summation.

She wrapped her arms around her middle. Her own disappointed shock at the news that her supposed suitor, Cecil Cooper, had just got engaged to Miss Dawson did not seem to signify to anyone. But for her part, Trinny was reeling.

What did I do wrong this time?

Her eyes filled with tears as a hot whirlwind of confusion churned in her heart and promptly turned to despair. *I really think he was my last hope.*

The reality sank in that having arrived at twenty-two, maybe she really *was* at her last prayer. *But why? I don't understand. I'm not that bad. Why doesn't anyone ever pick me?*

"George, Abigail is right. You really must do something," Mama insisted, her face etched with her permanent look of weary exasperation. She paused. "There's always Lord Tuttle," she said meaningfully to her husband.

"Oh, Papa, no!" Trinny gasped in revulsion and looked sharply at her mother.

"Yes, Papa! Do it, do it!" her younger sisters cheered. "Make her marry Tuttle the Tortoise!"

If the eligible bachelors of Moonlight Square only knew the designations the Glendon girls had dreamed up to keep them all straight...

"Oh, please keep your voices down, you mad tribe of Amazons. You're giving me a headache," Papa huffed.

"Girls, the neighbors will hear you!" Mama agreed.

But there was no quieting five opinionated young ladies when they felt the world had wronged them.

"It's a perfect match! The Tortoise is even odder than Trinny!" Gwendolyn said with a snicker.

"Then she can be Trinny, *Lady* Tortoise!" Jane burst out, pointing at her, rousing uproarious laughter from Betsy and titters from the rest.

Lord Beresford heaved a sigh and looked regretfully at his firstborn.

Trinny's eyes widened at his *I give up* glance. "Oh, Papa, you wouldn't!" she cried, while Abigail folded her arms across her chest and gave her a smug look.

Trinny threw up her hands. "The man takes a year to speak a sentence!"

"*And* he's bald," Betsy pointed out with a vengeful grin, as though it were only Trinny's rightful comeuppance for inconveniencing them all by driving her suitors away time after time with her impertinent remarks and odd topics of conversation.

Betsy turned to Mama. "Can I have her room once she's married off?"

Their dam ignored the little opportunist and endeavored to set her eldest straight. "Katrina, you've already had *four* Seasons, and now we're onto the fifth? This is getting a little ridiculous! What of all your sisters?"

The beautiful red-haired countess gestured at the rest of her brood, three of whom had already made their debuts. "Are they all to have the same? You'll put your father in the poor house!"

"I'd hardly say that," the earl muttered, then glanced grimly at his lady. "But if that is your wish, I will drop a hint to the baron tomorrow at the club."

Trinny swept the lot of them with an overwhelmed glance—and fled.

"Get back here this instant, young lady!" Mama ordered.

"Oh, leave her alone, Alice," Papa muttered.

"Girls, go to your rooms," was the last thing Trinny heard her mother say as she snatched the park key off its peg near the door before bursting out of the house.

Outside, the night's satin darkness blanketed Moonlight Square, hiding the tears that leaped into her eyes; she gulped for air as the late-April breeze tried to cool her burning cheeks.

The stars danced overhead and the plane trees swayed in the park across the street, but nothing could soothe away the sting of failing yet again to be chosen, wanted, desired…

Loved.

Wiping two tears quickly off her cheeks, she glanced up and down the street, but thankfully, none of her neighbors were out. She could not have borne to exchange niceties right now or answer questions like: *Wasn't Cecil Cooper courting you for a while there, dear?*

Oh, yes, ma'am! she would have barked at any nosy matron who might've asked the question of her right now. Which just went to show what a socially incompetent quiz she really was.

Her chin trembled and fresh tears jumped up into her eyes, exasperating her. *Blast it!*

Desperate to escape her own irksome life, Trinny ran down the few front steps of the Beresfords' elegant Town house, dashed across the quaint cobbled street, and fumbled to unlock the wrought iron gate to the private park that sat in the center of the garden square.

It would no doubt be deserted at this hour. It was open to the public during the day, but only the square's residents had keys to enjoy the park at night.

Whirling through the gate, she slammed it shut behind her with a satisfying bang and heard the lock click.

Ha. At least now her maddening family could not follow.

Legs still trembling beneath her, stomach in knots, she strode down the winding graveled path, the night breeze rippling through the tall, graceful branches overhead. A nightingale's lonely warbling and the perfume of the huge, mounded lilacs offered comfort, but when she came to the picturesque garden folly, she rushed up the few steps into it, crossed it, and paced twice back and forth, hands clenching and unclenching in dread and futile rage.

Then she leaned her back against one of the posts, buried her face in her hands…

And bawled.

# # #

Across the street from the garden square, the Grand Albion was lit up with its usual elegance—though not the famed Assembly Rooms on the upper floor, for it was merely Tuesday, not yet time for the essential Thursday night ball. Likewise, the few exclusive apartments on the top floor of the hotel were also quiet. But down on the ground level, the gentlemen's club in the back was lively with all the usual card games and billiards matches underway.

Gable Winston-McCray, Viscount Roland, heir to the Sefton earldom, smoked his cheroot and sipped his single malt Scotch, idly waiting for his turn to show his cards.

All the while, he listened in amusement to the banter among his club mates seated around the green baize table.

"But how the hell do you do it, Netherford? How does he always end up snaring every luscious new actress that prances onto the stage?"

"It's because he's a duke."

"And filthy rich."

"Oh, that has nothing to do with it, I assure you," Netherford drawled with a wicked smirk, then won another hand.

Gaelen Foley

"Bastard," Gable muttered good-naturedly, shoving his chips toward the dark-haired duke yet again.

Just then, one of the club's liveried footmen came speeding over to Gable with a silver tray. "Lord Roland. This just came for you, sir."

Gable looked at the note lying there on the tray and heaved a sigh. "If this is from my father, I am going to scream. Fair warning, lads."

He did not scream, as it turned out. He read the brief note, arched a brow, and murmured, "Hmm."

"Something wrong, Rollo?" his friend Lord Sidney asked.

"Ah, I have to go. Something I need to take care of."

"For Papa?" Netherford goaded him.

"For a lady," he replied with an equally wicked smile.

"Aha. Now that's the kind of summons I like getting at this hour," Netherford said.

Lord Tuttle huffed. "You good-looking bastards annoy the rest of us to no end," he grumbled.

"Sorry," Gable said dryly. He rose, then downed the last of his Scotch. "Evening, lads."

"Don't do anything I wouldn't do," Netherford called.

Sidney scoffed. "And what might that leave out, exactly?"

Their banter faded as Gable marched off on his mission. It wasn't quite what his friends had assumed, but the frantic note from Lady Hayworth did touch upon their assignation of earlier that day.

> You must find it at once and get it back to me! My husband gave me those earrings. If one turns up missing, he'll fly into a rage!

Unconcerned about old Hayworth or his drunken temper, Gable strolled out of the club into the agreeable spring night, then narrowed his eyes as he gazed across the street at the garden square. He walked over to the shoulder-high wrought iron fence around the park.

He did not feel like running home to get his park key, so he clenched his cheroot between his teeth, took off his tailcoat, and vaulted over the fence, landing in the park. Slinging his coat over his shoulder, he tucked a hand in his pocket and strolled back to the scene of his tryst with the infamously willing Lady Hayworth that afternoon. A quick romp in the garden folly had taken quite the edge off.

He was bemused to hear she had lost the earring, for that matter, since they had barely undressed. There had been no need, with her sitting on his lap, both of them swept up in the cheap thrill of maybe getting caught. The only real surprise was that he hadn't accidentally swallowed the thing.

Gable suddenly stopped short when he stepped around a bend in the winding path and the gazebo came into view.

Occupied.

His eyes narrowed, and his brow slowly furrowed as his gaze homed in on some poor female sobbing her heart out there.

Bloody hell.

Gingerly venturing closer, he softened his steps so the gravel wouldn't crunch. It felt wrong to invade her grief, whoever she was.

I could wait, he thought. *Finish my cheroot. Maybe she's almost done.*

But future earls didn't like waiting, as a rule.

He took another drag, frowned to note that his cheroot was down to a nub anyway, then tossed it down and crushed it out under the heel of his new boot, unsure how to proceed.

Wonder what's so wrong, he thought. Then it occurred to him that if the woman accidentally found the diamond first, she might try to claim it. He had no intention of buying his paramour another, so he concluded, *I'll just try not to disturb her.*

As he walked on, her crying grew louder. Her shoulders shook, and he felt a tug of amused sympathy. *Poor thing.* As he neared, the moonlight gleamed off her smooth, shiny, pale-red hair, alerting him that she must be one of Lord Beresford's daughters.

How many of them there were exactly, Gable did not know. He could not tell the lot of pretty little redheads apart. Nor had he tried.

It was not wise for a dedicated rakehell to stare overlong at the daughters of a neighboring lord, unless he wished to have a bride thrust upon him.

Which Gable wanted like a hole in the head, so he kept his eyes to himself whenever he saw them.

Impatient to get his task over with, he cleared his throat as politely as possible. "Ahem."

# # #

Pretty well cried out by now, Trinny looked up abruptly. Her swollen eyes widened as she spotted the tall, broad-shouldered figure standing in the moonlight.

Oh, just when I thought I could not be any more humiliated.

The dashing fellow sauntered forward down the path with a suave air, his coat slung over his shoulder.

"I say," he called in a deep voice as breezy as the night, "sorry to bother you, but it seems a lady friend of mine dropped an earring here earlier today. She's quite frantic to have it back, so if you don't mind, I should like to have a quick look round. This will only take a minute." He hesitated. "Er, carry on."

Carry on? Trinny stiffened with indignation.

She drew herself up, mortified at being found weeping like a watering pot. "No matter. I shall go," she said in a brittle tone, lifting her head and avoiding the gentleman's curious gaze in her embarrassment.

She marched across the gazebo to leave as the intruder was arriving, but when their paths crossed on the painted steps, two things happened.

One: He offered her his handkerchief.

"Here," he said softly. "You look like you could use this."

Two: She lifted her chin with a frosty air to decline his pity with what was left of her pride, and seeing him up close, she recognized the man.

Lord Sweet Cheeks!

Well, that was his name to the Glendon girls, anyway, and it had nothing to do with his strikingly handsome face.

Trinny jolted back a bit in surprise—and nearly tumbled onto her derriere, naturally, as a result of forgetting she was standing on steps. Instantly, his hand shot out and he steadied her with a firm grasp on her arm.

"Easy, there," he chided, smooth as silk.

God, I am a quiz, she concluded in despair.

"Thank you." She gazed for a moment at his steely jawline, his loose fall of dark, glossy hair, and most especially, his sculpted mouth.

She quickly looked away and accepted his handkerchief to try to cover her awkwardness.

"You all right?" he asked.

"Oh, I'm just wonderful, thanks," she muttered.

He stared at her as though she were a puzzle that he really didn't have that much interest in putting together. Shrugging off a wisp of curiosity, he tilted his head and gave her a charmingly cordial smile; at that, Trinny abruptly realized she was in his way.

He was waiting for her to step aside so he could search the gazebo for the missing item, as he had stated.

She did so, still clutching his handkerchief as the handsome rogue brushed by her. She turned to watch him pass. There was a reason, after all, that she and her sisters had mischievously named him Lord Sweet Cheeks.

My, my. The chap knew how to fill out a pair of pantaloons.

They had quite a few neighbors of his ilk here in Moonlight Square. Dashing, gloriously handsome rakehells, highborn bachelors all, who never looked twice at her or most eligible young misses, for that matter.

Wealthy, loose-living rogues who Mama said had to be physically dragged to the altar. In truth, Trinny did not hold these idle hedonists in the highest of esteem.

They were overgrown boys, in her view, the centers of their own worlds, living for the moment, chasing their pleasures all over Town.

Admittedly, they were nice to look at.

"Whatever it is, you know," he suddenly offered, "it'll be all right." He paused in hunting around the floor of the gazebo to send her a brief, reassuring smile.

Trinny's heart quaked.

When she noticed that his eyes were kinder than she had expected, she could not help lingering on the gazebo steps for a moment to acknowledge the embarrassing state in which he'd found her.

"I'm not…usually such a watering pot."

"I didn't see anything. Don't fret, my lady. I am the soul of discretion, believe me." The words sounded wry, laden with sardonic meaning just beneath the surface.

He sent her a conspiratorial wink and turned away, continuing his search. He tossed his coat over the railing of the garden folly and crouched down to peer through a crack in the floorboards.

Trinny's brow puckered with wariness as she watched him. If she were seen out here alone with the likes of him, she could be ruined.

Then again, did it even matter anymore? Would anybody even care?

The thought made fresh tears well up in her eyes, but she refused to be dragged down into self-pity, and blew her nose on his handkerchief.

The sophisticated viscount looked up in surprise, as though he'd never heard a lady really blow her nose before.

Trinny didn't care. There was no point in trying to impress the likes of Lord Sweet Cheeks. No point ruing the fact that their beautiful stallion of a neighbor had no doubt noticed her odd ways from the first instant he'd laid eyes on her sobbing like a cake head.

Why worry? She already knew full well she didn't have a chance with a blue-ribbon stud. In truth, it came as a relief, not having to try for once. Not having to hold the teeth-gritting smile of a debutante and pretend to laugh at things that weren't funny. Not having to watch the sweets at balls go by on footmen's trays and never gobble down a one, all the while being laced into stays to smash her figure into shape.

All Mama's rules for catching husbands... They didn't really seem to work, she mused. Then the thought of going home to that madhouse made her turn to Lord Sweet Cheeks.

"An earring, you say?" she asked with a last, brisk sniffle, tucking his handkerchief into her pocket. "What does it look like? I'll help you find it."

"Why, that's very neighborly of you," he said in surprise, looking askance at her. "Diamond chandelier of some sort, apparently."

"Oh." She nodded. "Well, the moonlight ought to help."

"Moonlight always helps." He sent her another knowing, wistful smile.

She returned it ruefully, aware he was alluding to her tears. "I suppose it does, a bit."

Then she turned away and lifted the hem of her skirts as she stepped down off the garden folly stairs, joining the hunt in that area.

While she crouched down and searched the flowerbeds beside the gazebo stairs for any promising sparkle in the dirt, she noticed, out of the corner of her eye, that Lord Roland was studying her.

"So why the tears?" he asked after a moment, as though he could not resist.

She sent him a dubious glance, and one of her infamous "odd duck" questions escaped her. "Why do you want to know? So you can gossip about me?"

"I don't gossip." He scowled. "Suit yourself, then. I only asked to pass the time. You don't have to help me—"

"I don't fancy going home right now. I might as well."

He shrugged off her answer and resumed his search, now looking slightly offended.

Trinny's heart sank. *There you go again. Being quarrelsome with men.*

"I got some bad news tonight, is all," she offered after a brief pause.

Hunting under the bench that ran around the perimeter of the gazebo's interior, he glanced over at her curiously. "Sorry to hear it. Someone die?"

"Oh, no. Not that bad." Trinny heaved a sigh. "I just found out tonight that someone I thought was courting me has got engaged to someone else."

He straightened up and turned to her indignantly. "Bounder led you on?" he asked, bristling.

"No, I wouldn't say *that*," she answered, a bit startled by his emphatic response. "I probably just deluded myself into thinking he was even interested in the first place. He was probably just being polite. And wondering what planet I came from," she said under her breath.

"Really?" His lips quirked in amusement, and the dear fellow attempted to rouse a smile out of her. "Well, this is very exciting for me. I've never met a lady from another planet before."

"Ha-ha," she replied.

"Which one? You must tell me, for I'm something of an amateur astronomer. I even have a telescope. So tell me of your homeland. I do hope it's Saturn. I love all those dramatic rings. I have a theory that they're horseracing tracks. Am I right?"

She smiled at him. "Are you trying to cheer me up?"

He smiled back. "Is it working?"

She nodded with a slight blush.

"I really do have a telescope, though," he informed her. "I find the sciences rather interesting."

She looked at him in surprise. "So do I."

"No, you don't. You're a girl."

She arched a brow at him and shrugged. "Yes, but I'm an odd duck, you see, and something of a bluestocking. So I'm told."

"A bluestocking who just got her heart broken, hmm?" he replied as he came down from the gazebo and began searching the next flowerbed around the white lattice-clad foundations of the garden folly.

"I don't know." Trinny shook her head. "The truth is...I didn't even like him very much. Maybe that's why it stings."

He stopped and looked at her. "Because you were willing to marry him if he had asked?"

She just looked at him, then bit her lip in guilty silence.

Lord Roland shuddered seemingly down to his bones at her answer.

Taken aback, Trinny felt her cheeks flood with heat at the genuine disapproval emanating from the bachelor at her willingness to marry a fellow she didn't love.

She couldn't believe it. A rakehell of his ilk, judging *her*? Of all the

Gaelen Foley

nerve!

"I have a duty to my family!" she informed him.

"Oh, I understand completely," he replied. "I have a father who badgers me constantly about preserving the almighty family line. That doesn't mean I give in to it. Miss…?"

"*Lady* Katrina Glendon," she corrected with a smirk, annoyed. "As in, the eldest. I have a houseful of younger sisters who cannot marry until I get out of the way. But that is proving to be something of a problem."

"Why?" he demanded, flicking a glance over her that was not unadmiring.

But she was too embarrassed to recognize the compliment, and huffed at him. "Nosy, aren't you? Humph. Why don't *you* answer a question this time? Whose earring are we looking for?" she asked knowingly.

"Er," he said.

"As I thought. So don't send me your disapproval, sir. I know what goes on," she said sagely, then continued looking.

The twist of his lips seemed to suggest he found her assurance of worldly wisdom terribly amusing. "Well, I'm sorry if I offended you with the question, Lady Katrina. It just seems strange, that's all." He glanced her over again, taking a closer look, almost rudely. "I'm something of an expert on the fair sex, and I don't see anything particularly wrong with you. So what seems to be the problem?"

She looked over at him with another slight huff, still on her knees in the grass at the edge of the flowerbed.

"What?" he asked.

"You're very blunt, aren't you?"

"Not usually. I feel bad you were crying." He shrugged. "Just trying to help."

"Why?" she asked in suspicion.

"Because you're helping me—obviously!" he pointed out, nodding at the flowerbeds. "But suit yourself. If you don't wish to talk about it, I hardly care."

Despite his words, he clearly seemed miffed at her rejection of his offer of a willing ear. Trinny looked at him in astonishment. God, he was more of an oddment than she was, him and his science jokes. Who'd have thought it?

"Fine," she said. "You really want to know?"

"Not really. I don't care, as I told you." He shrugged, but she knew better.

"Whenever I think a chap might like me—because sometimes, they actually almost do—I get so nervous I start bumbling like a nincompoop. I make bad jokes. I ask the same question twice in a row because I forget what they just told me. I say things that accidentally insult them, and somehow…" She sighed. "I ruin it every time."

He was silent for a moment, hunting among the flowerbeds. "Well, there's a simple explanation."

"There is?"

"You undermine yourself unwittingly," he said with a shrewd glance at her, "because it isn't what you want."

His low-toned observation struck her with the force of an arrow to the heart. Her defenses recoiled. "Oh, you think I do it on purpose?"

"Hit a nerve?" he asked softly.

"You think I *like* being lonely? You think it feels very good not having anybody want me? But, you… Look at you. How could *you* possibly understand that?"

"Because I do the same thing," he replied.

She blinked. "You…? How?"

"Chase the wrong women. My father tells me so. But the truth is, I'm well aware. You want to know what I think?"

"I think you're going to tell me either way."

He turned to her. "The problem isn't *us*. The problem is this whole blasted business of marriage."

"How do you mean?"

"Well, the whole thing's insane, inn't it?" he declared. "Who wants to end up locked in a cage with someone who despises you?" He scowled, pausing. "The earring we're looking for belongs to someone in that situation. I would hate to see you end up like her. So take my advice—I'll give it to you because you seem like a nice girl. If there's not a man out there who wants to make you happy, then make *yourself* happy, and let 'em all go hang."

Her eyes widened slowly.

"That's what I'd do, anyway," he added.

When she finally recovered from her shock at his defiance, she couldn't help but scoff. "Well, all that's easy for you to say. You're a man. Lack of marriage doesn't mean social death for your kind. For us, it's…" She made a slicing gesture across her throat.

His eyes twinkled as he gazed at her. "You *are* a quiz, aren't you?"

"I told you."

He grinned. "I kind of like it."

She eyed him distrustfully as a fond, quiet laugh escaped him, then he kept looking.

Unsure what to make of her new friend, she continued poking among the pansies, hellebores, and all the way back to the tall foxglove, very much hoping that she didn't accidentally touch a spider.

They fell silent as they searched.

Suddenly, right at the base of the gazebo, Trinny spotted something shimmering in the dirt. She carefully reached between the cool, succulent leaves of some daffodils, and her fingers closed around the sharp edges of the jewel.

"Found it!" With a beaming grin, she picked it up and brushed the soil off it, examining the earring. "Oh, that's beautiful."

"Yes."

"Here." But when she turned to offer it to him, Lord Roland wasn't looking at the sparkly diamonds.

He was staring right at *her*.

Trinny instantly felt self-conscious. "What? Did I say something daft? Because I didn't even notice if I—"

"No." He tilted his head, studying her intently and making no move to take the jewel.

She eyed him. "Uh, what's wrong?"

He spoke abruptly after a pause. "My lady, I know you're not interested in me, nor do I want you to be, but after all you've been through, I think there's something you need to know…and something I'd like to do."

"What's that?" she asked, puzzled.

"This." He took her chin between his thumb and finger, and gently tilted her face upward as he leaned down, lowering his head.

Trinny gasped just a little as his lips alighted on hers. She went very still, her heart pounding loud enough to be heard in the Midlands. The light pressure of his warm, satin mouth became a caress, with the barest hint of a world of masterful skill beyond it.

Though brief, his gentle kiss left her dizzied on her knees beside him on the grass. When it ended, a long, dreamy second passed before she could open her eyes.

"Is this you chasing the wrong women again?" she breathed.

"No. This is me proving a point."

She lifted her lashes and stared at him, slightly entranced. "What point is that?"

"Ah, you didn't get it," he whispered. "Let's try that again." This time, his arm wrapped around her waist; he pulled her firmly against his lean, much larger body, and his kiss deepened, coaxing her lips apart.

The earring dropped from her grasp. If it was lost again, well, so was she. Astonishment, perhaps, kept her from protesting while his tongue swirled in her mouth, enthralling her, and a hundred realizations eddied through her mind.

So this is what a rake's kiss tastes like. Liquor and danger and smoke, while the pleasant roughness of his day's beard chafed against her chin.

Her hand slid up his chest to his shoulder, in search of something solid to cling to, for his embrace made her want to melt onto her back in the cool spring grass. She wasn't even sure when she'd begun actively returning his kiss, seeking more of it, and trying things, instead of merely accepting its deep, luscious rhythm.

But then the *other* realization floated in. *Hmm, so this is why young ladies aren't left alone with rakehells.*

Ack! What am I doing?

When her senses came back in a rush, she nearly threw her neck out, pulling back violently, the dangerous taste of him on her tongue, the scent of his cologne on her clothes.

"How dare you?" she panted in rather feigned, belated outrage.

He arched a brow, his eyes afire, chest heaving.

"I mean—what do you think you're doing?" she demanded a little less emphatically.

"My dear young lady," he ground out, "if you still didn't get it, you're not a quiz. You're an idiot."

She huffed with still-dazed indignation. But when he rose from his knees and offered her a gentlemanly hand up, Trinny found herself briefly on eye level with the front portion of his tight pantaloons.

Good God! All thoughts promptly flew out of her head.

Because the effect that their kiss had made on his…his person, she thought, was abundantly obvious. Indeed, it was right in front of her face.

And then, slowly, she got the point he had been making.

"Ohh," she whispered, blushing scarlet as she whipped her gaze up to meet his uncertainly.

He stared down at her matter-of-factly, looking more amused than embarrassed that she had seen the great, manly swelling.

Well, the rogue had cause to look proud, she supposed, while he stood there waiting, hand outstretched, to pull her to her feet.

Trinny accepted his help but was still speechless.

Too abashed to meet his gaze, she busied herself dusting the bits of grass and dirt off her skirts.

Lord Roland bent down and picked up the earring from where she had dropped it. He straightened up, tossed it lightly, and caught it in his hand, then tucked the bauble into his breast pocket. He cleared his throat wryly and adjusted his nether regions, turning away.

"Well, then!" he said. "Good night, my lady. Nice meeting you." With that, he went and collected his tailcoat from the railing.

Trinny marveled at his splendid composure, given her own quasi-hysteria. She was still standing there, at a loss, exactly where he'd left her, when he sauntered across the gazebo and looked down over the railing at her.

"Do you need me to walk you home?" he asked.

She shook her head dazedly, wide-eyed.

He searched her face, his own chiseled and princely in the moonlight. "You're sure?"

Mute, she nodded.

"All right, then, if you're sure. Thanks for the help." His lips twisted. "And the kiss."

She bit her lip, for the word alone made her rather crave more of his mouth.

"Ciao, bella." He slung the tailcoat over his shoulder as before and strolled away.

Perhaps proximity to that man had clouded her mind, for it wasn't until he was several yards away that she found her tongue and her wits again.

She walked around from the back of the gazebo to the front, brow furrowed, fists bunched at her sides. "I am not a charity case, you know!"

"Absolutely not. I believe you noticed how much I enjoyed that."

A fresh burst of flame shot into her cheeks, burning in the cool night air.

"You didn't have to kiss me just to make a point," she called after him, taking care to sound indignant, though she was unsure herself if she was angry or secretly delighted.

She heard his wicked laugh in the darkness. "Oh yes, I did. Believe me."

She refused to smile at his flattering jest, throwing up her hands. "Why can't a man just *say* things? You know, with *words*?"

He cast an extremely roguish glance over his shoulder and merely called, "Go home! Your parents will worry!"

Oh, you cheeky thing, she thought, shaking her head and trembling with confusion and excitement as he disappeared amid the park shadows.

Well, at least he got what he came for. She, however, had got a great deal more than she had bargained for.

Egads, he's right. I'd better head home. She had lost all track of time and had no idea how long she had been out there. She blew out a steadying exhalation, then ran a hand over her hair in case he had mussed it.

Blazes, never in her life had she imagined she would ever be the sort of girl who engaged in passionate kisses with a stranger in—let alone *behind*—a garden folly. Yet she had to admit it had been exciting, and he had certainly cheered her up. But he had shown her something important in the process, too. Something that made her square her shoulders and lift her chin as she headed homeward.

Lord Roland had proved to her that, despite her lack of success in the love department—and after so much painful rejection had eroded her confidence—all hope was not lost. To be sure, he was not on the marriage mart himself, which was a little disappointing, but at least he had been totally honest about that. The important thing was that, oh yes, she had got the message quite clearly: She *was* beautiful. She *was* a desirable woman.

It was his own seductive way of telling her not to worry—some man out there would eventually want her.

After all, *he* did.

Though this was wildly flattering, not to mention a sweet, unexpected balm to her much-bruised heart, it lit a sudden spark of rebellion deep in her core. Maybe it was contagious, and she had caught it from him.

But honestly, if someone that delicious could genuinely want me, then maybe there's nothing wrong with me at all. And if not, then why the devil am I putting myself through all this?

She paused mid-stride on the path home, as though struck by a thunderbolt. Maybe the problem really was marriage, not her.

Oh, what a boon it would be to stop agonizing over it. Having her pride trampled continually, putting herself through this torture, all to win a prize she didn't even want!

Hope soared through her, greater even than when Cecil Cooper had asked her to go out on a drive with him in his open carriage in Hyde Park. Maybe there *was* some way she could just embrace her spinsterhood and…what had the rogue said?

Make *herself* happy.

She shivered at the revolutionary notion, unsure. To her ears, it sounded a bit like giving up. It sounded like defeat. But to her heart, it felt like victory, and to her soul, it felt like freedom.

Stop trying to get a husband?

Her tears long gone, a tremulous smile spread across her face. Oh, to be free of that burden. To tell her parents she just couldn't do it anymore, that she was stepping aside, giving up her privilege as the eldest to let Abigail marry her Freddie, and so be it.

Perhaps she'd taken leave of her senses, but what a relief it would be, not having to go through that anymore. Just to be left alone to discover who she *was* when she wasn't trying to mold herself into whatever some eligible bachelor on Mama's list wanted.

She bit her lip at the hopeful possibility, as dangerous and thrilling as Lord Roland himself. Of course, Mama would have an apoplectic fit…

But Trinny suddenly didn't care.

It wasn't Mama's life. *She* wasn't the one who'd have to suffer. Trinny shook her head in wonder as the moon shone down and the starlight danced on her skin.

I can't believe it, but maybe he's right. If those men don't want me, let 'em all go hang.

Without warning, she threw her arms up in silent exultation and clenched her fists in freedom as a grin of victory burst across her face. *Yes, I'm going to do it.*

To hell with them all!

CHAPTER 2

We Meet Again

The next time she saw him was ten days—or rather, nights—later. The tail end of April had given way to May, and the Season had started in earnest. Trinny was saying goodbye to her friend Felicity Carvel at only the second of the famous Thursday night balls held throughout the Season at the Grand Albion.

Her family never missed them, but this one was particularly special, given Abigail and Freddie's big announcement.

Felicity glanced worriedly at the wall clock, then frowned at Trinny in concern. "It's eleven, so my great-aunt wants to go. But I don't feel like I should leave you."

"I'm perfectly fine," she assured the regal blonde. Trinny smiled with determination that it should be so. "I'm happy for my sister. And as for me, this was the right decision."

Felicity did not look entirely convinced. Her sea-green eyes were full of worry as she searched Trinny's face. But then, the prim-and-proper Miss Carvel was always slightly worried about someone—if not the elderly dragon aunt she attended, then her swashbuckling elder brother.

The utterly delicious Major Peter Carvel—Danger Man, to the Glendon girls—had helped Welly crush Napoleon, and then, having survived the war, Major Carvel had promptly gone sailing off to risk his neck again. This time, he was on some exciting expedition exploring remote tropical mountain forests in India amongst the elephants and tigers, and, supposedly, mysterious tribes of headhunters who dwelled in the jungles far beyond the reach of the civilized Hindus.

Major Carvel's ilk considered such suicidal ventures *fun*. Perhaps he was mad, Trinny mused. No doubt her friend had cause to worry.

"Oh, Mrs. Brown is waving to me," Felicity said, waving back to the plump, matronly widow who lived with her and her great-aunt in Mayfair and helped care for the old dragon. "I'm sorry, I really have to go. Are you sure you'll be all right?"

"I'm fine! I told you."

"Too bad, I do love this song." Felicity glanced wistfully over her shoulder at the dance floor as the orchestra started playing another set. She sighed at having to leave early, as usual, keeping company with old ladies, but far be it from her to complain.

"I'll walk you out," Trinny said. She had no desire to watch Cecil Cooper dancing with his new fiancée or to stand alone by the wall while her younger sister skipped off with her beau, too.

"Oh, thanks!" Felicity said. "I think my aunt would like a word with you, anyway."

"Uh-oh," Trinny murmured with a knowing smile.

"I fear Her Ladyship has some advice for you."

"No doubt."

Felicity stifled a laugh, then they wove through the crowded ballroom toward the open double doors, dodging busy liveried footmen delivering drinks on trays. They had to fight against the tide of couples rushing to join the contredanse before it was too late.

Even Trinny's parents were out there.

As she escorted her friend toward the exit, she could not fail to notice, by the brilliance of the chandeliers, certain pitying looks and head shakes from her neighbors here and there. But she flashed a bright, confident smile at the lot of them as she passed, determined to make them see she was not concerned about her future in the slightest.

Felicity suddenly gasped. "Oh God, she's on the steps! Excuse me!" The normally demure girl began shoving people aside to dash protectively to the aid of her elderly kinswoman.

To be sure, the sweeping marble staircase that curved down into the entrance hall could have proved a danger to a frail-boned lady of advanced age who walked with a cane, no matter how much of a spitfire she might be.

While Felicity hurried into position to assist Her Ladyship down the steps, Trinny followed, rather wishing she could've told her friend about the kiss she had shared with Lord Roland less than a fortnight ago.

But it was probably best to be discreet. Her friend did tend to be a little straitlaced, and Trinny wasn't sure what Felicity might think of her for letting him do that to her. She did not wish to alienate a comrade now that she had just found her way back into her sisters' graces.

For, oh, yes, to her own surprise, and after much brooding on the matter, Trinny had decided to take the rakehell's advice. As she followed her friend out of the ballroom, she mentally reviewed how it had all unfolded...

A couple of days after the kiss, she had called her parents together into the drawing room to have *the talk* with them, while her sisters eavesdropped outside the closed door.

"Ahem. Mama, Papa: I have made a decision," she had said calmly and with great composure. She had then lifted up the prop she had prepared for the demonstration.

A neat white spinster's cap.

She had adorned it herself with a fringe of white eyelet and a small blue ribbon tied around the crown. "Some women clearly are not meant to be married," she had told them. "And I cannot stand in the way of my sister's happiness anymore. So I'm afraid you must pardon me from the so-called necessity of finding a husband. I do not wish to marry," she had declared. "I will undertake to pay you back slowly for the expenses I incurred with my unnecessary Seasons, for I do not wish to be a burden on the family, either now or in the future."

Mama's mouth was already hanging open, but Papa had blustered at once that she was nothing of the kind. Trinny had rushed on before she lost her nerve. "I have devised a simple and ladylike way to bolster my own income henceforth. I will discreetly sell the hats I design to a few of the better milliner's shops."

Mama had covered her mouth in horror; Papa's jaw had now dropped, too.

Trinny had quickly hastened on to conclude her explanation. "You know I'm very fond of fashioning hats for my own amusement. Don't worry, no one need find out that I'm selling them. Well, unless they become all the rage, then we can tell!"

Of course, not everyone appreciated her style of millinery.

"The important thing is, my dear esteemed parents, I wish to be an independent lady, free of husbands. I do not fear this fate. I do not scorn it. I embrace it happily."

Just like Sweet Cheeks had said.

"Others may look askance on me in Society, but I care not. I would rather live alone than be locked in a cage with someone I don't love. And you see, this will benefit the both of you," she hastened to point out. "Because this way, I'll be here to take care of you when you're old."

"Oh, Trinny," Mama had uttered in shock at last, her face resembling the theatre mask of tragedy. "I'm a failure as a mother."

"No, you should be happy for me, Mama!" Trinny had scolded with a cheerful smile. "*I'm* happy! This is so much better for me, please. I am tired of being told in so many words by all these stupid men that I'm not worth choosing. That I am not worth loving. I know this to be false. So I'm choosing myself! And so…"

With a humorous air of great ceremony, she had donned the cute spinster's cap and lifted her chin proudly.

"Isn't it pretty?"

Then Mama fainted.

Not that it was terribly unusual for her to do so. Sometimes the Glendon girls even suspected that she faked it for effect.

As for Papa, while Trinny waited with a heart-pounding gulp, to see if she had her sire's permission, a broad, proud smile had slowly spread across the earl's face.

He had a twinkle of amusement in his eyes, as though he knew something she had not yet grasped. The earl had glanced at his countess, and seeing she had swooned back safely onto the couch, he had stood up, walked over and taken Trinny's face between his hands, placing a gentle kiss upon her forehead.

"You are a wonderful young woman," he had murmured. "Those of us with eyes can see that in an instant. You have my blessing, but only because I cannot bear to see you wounded anymore. I love you."

"So…you won't make me marry Tuttle the Tortoise?"

"Of course not," he had whispered. "He's not worthy of you." Then he had hugged her, and Trinny nearly wept at his tender words of support. Things might have been different, she had mused, if she could have found a man out there as kind as her papa.

Alas, her dam was considerably less understanding about matters. Once they had revived her, Trinny sat beside her mother, holding both her hands and reminding her how exciting it was going to be, now that she could start planning Abby's wedding.

That had abruptly stopped her tears. It was no secret in their house, after all, that Abby had always been Mama's favorite. When Trinny's news was shared with her sisters, there had been nearly as much weeping with joy as there had been angry tears of a few nights ago.

In any case, a stately voice ahead suddenly yanked her out of her thoughts.

"Lady Katrina! A word with you, please," said Her Ladyship, still hobbling down the steps. "Where is the gel? Daydreaming?"

"Oh, she's right here, Aunt." Felicity sent Trinny a *snap to it* glance at the summons from Lady Kirby.

"Coming!" Trinny lifted the hem of her skirts a little to hasten down a few more steps so she might appear before the grand dame.

Her Ladyship was proceeding slowly and methodically, her cane thumping on the stairs with each step. Holding on to the banister with one hand and her cane with the other, while Mrs. Brown walked slowly beside her and Felicity trailed behind, the old woman descended at a snail's pace. But although the dowager was frail of body, she had great force of mind.

"Yes, ma'am? You wished to speak to me?" Trinny inquired.

"I have a few thoughts pertaining to your situation," the old dragon informed her.

Felicity sent Trinny a discreet, mirthful smile from behind Her Ladyship.

"Slaves of convention will no doubt say you have thrown away your life, but I see matters differently. As I do with most things," Lady Kirby added with a sharp stare.

Trinny's mouth quirked; she was heartened to know she was not the only eccentric here tonight. The slight arch of Her Ladyship's silvery eyebrow communicated her awareness that the two of them were not so different.

"It is an interesting choice you have made, gel. You must come to call on me soon. I have some ideas regarding how you might take best advantage of your newfound freedom. For you see, I was in a situation somewhat resembling your own for many years, indeed, most of my life."

"Really?"

"Oh yes. I had a husband once, very long ago. I barely remember what he looked like, but I loved him dearly at the time, and then he died." She sighed but shrugged off her ancient loss as she continued clumping slowly down the stairs. "We scarcely had a decade together."

"I'm very sorry," Trinny offered.

"That's not the point. Though Kirby is long gone, he left me all his money. He was a nabob, you know," she added with a twinkle in her eyes. "He died before we ever had children. Everyone around me pitied me so much for that—well, except for some nephew of my husband's, who inherited his title as a result. But I have had a very interesting life even so, and I would encourage you to seek the same, however possible. I try to tell my niece this, as well, but alas, she's terribly conventional."

"Ma'am!" Felicity said indignantly.

"You know it's quite true, Felicity. Now then, Lady Katrina, when you come to my house, I shall give you a list of suggestions I think you'll find agreeable. With that horrid war finally over, the Continent is open to travelers, and *I* say, get you to France." She winked at her. "Italy, Spain, Greece, Portugal…"

"Er, that sounds very exciting, my lady. Of course, I can't really do any traveling until my sister's wedding passes."

"Mmm." Lady Kirby conceded this with a regretful nod. "How I wish I could go there again…"

All of a sudden, the double front doors to the marble entrance hall below burst open, and a crowd of rakehells poured in from the windy night outside.

They traveled in a pack, like wolves. They were rowdy and loud, fashionable and merry, windblown and more than a little tipsy, one more handsome than the next.

From the corner of her eye, Trinny saw Felicity flinch when the ringleader of their set swaggered in: the tall, handsome Duke of Netherford. Trinny's own breath caught when she spotted Lord Roland among the pack of pretty fellows.

Promptly, her heart began to race. It was a foolish reaction, no doubt, but it couldn't be helped. When a young lady shared a kiss in the moonlight with a dashing stranger—her first kiss, at that—it must understandably have at least *some* lingering effect.

Hiding her reaction as best she could, she ran her hand along the smooth hardwood of the banister, grateful for how it steadied her, as the sight of him made her slightly dizzy. She bit her lip at his striking good looks, the white flash of his teeth as he laughed at something one of his friends said. His tall, elegantly muscled form was lean and hard, as she well remembered when she'd been crushed against him, and she could see that his smooth, shiny hair was not just dark but a dramatic ebony.

She still had no idea what color his eyes were, though…

Quickly stopping herself from staring, she looked away and

wondered where the gentlemen had been. Their set always came late. But on second thought, maybe she didn't want to know. It was probably someplace disreputable.

A few of the young men spotted Lady Kirby coming down the steps, but Naughty Netherford's gaze traveled past the old woman and clamped on to Felicity. Trinny saw him give a slight jolt and freeze briefly as he caught sight of the blonde. *Well, well.*

Trinny knew the duke was a longtime friend of the Carvel family. Indeed, he was funding Major Carvel's current expedition. So it didn't make much sense to Trinny why Felicity always turned her *most* prim and proper whenever the so-called Duke of Scandal came into sight, considering she'd known him all her life.

For his part, seeing Felicity seemed to put a damper on Netherford's rakish swagger. He offered the blonde a respectful nod from across the room, and then glanced at Lady Kirby and seemed to note her difficulty in coming down the stairs.

Turning away, the notoriously wicked duke clapped one of his friends on the shoulder, murmured something, pointed to another one of the men, and nodded toward the staircase.

Trinny did not know the two young rakehells who came bounding up the steps, but Lady Kirby burst out laughing and scolded the lads simultaneously as they surrounded her, declaring themselves on a mission.

"We shall carry you, my lady!"

"It would be our honor!"

Trinny got out of the way, but Felicity practically yelped as the two young lords clasped arms, bent down, and fashioned a queen's seat for the dowager to sit on.

"Oh my God!" Felicity uttered, thunderstruck, as they proceeded to carry the old girl away. "They're drunk! They'll drop her!"

Mrs. Brown looked aghast, as well. But Lady Kirby was delighted, her bony hands planted on the broad shoulders of the two rascals who'd been sent to convey her smoothly down the rest of the steps, easing her long, painful journey.

The rest of the rogues applauded and hooted for their feat, and Lady Kirby laughed like a debutante.

"Ah, that's sweet," Trinny murmured.

But Felicity sent her a scowl, her lips pursed. Clutching her heart, she sent the Duke of Netherford a glare, which he either ignored or simply missed due to the fact that a flurry of ladies had come running to greet him and the other new arrivals. But mostly him.

"I'd better go," Felicity said in a taut voice, then hurried down the rest of the staircase to attend her aunt.

Trinny went with her. Lady Kirby was now safely down the stairs; the rogues were gently setting her on her feet on the marble floor. All the young men were joking with her, for she was a great favorite with them for her unconventional views, and because she occasionally gambled with them. Clearly loving all the attention, she poked blond, charming Lord Sidney in the backside with her cane.

He yelped and whipped around. "You vixen! What was that for?"

"You were in my way," the dowager informed him calmly.

He narrowed his cobalt eyes at her in playful warning. "I think I know better."

"Look at her, having the time of her life," Felicity muttered. "Shameless."

"Not that one can blame her," Trinny said, looking askance at her disapproving friend.

Felicity faltered, though, as she neared Netherford, who was greeting Her Ladyship. "You're looking well, ma'am." He then offered Felicity a polite but highly cautious smile. "Miss Carvel."

"Your Grace." Her wide-eyed stare at the large, dark-haired man softened a little, seemingly in spite of herself. "Perfect timing, as usual," she added.

His brown eyes searched hers with pensive regret. "We're always missing each other somehow," he said in a surprisingly gentle tone.

But Trinny furrowed her brow, watching their exchange. If His Grace really wanted to see Felicity, all he had to do was come to the ball on time.

Her friend seemed to flounder, nodded, and dropped her gaze. "Indeed. Good evening." Clearing her throat, Felicity mumbled good night to him, waved to Trinny, and then stepped outside while Mrs. Brown tried to coax Her Ladyship toward the exit as well.

"Come, Aunt, our coach is waiting!" Felicity said impatiently, peering in again after a moment.

"That girl really needs to relax," Lord Roland remarked as he sauntered toward Trinny with a lazy smile.

"Pardon, that *girl* is my friend," she chided playfully, though her heart beat faster as he neared.

"It's nevertheless true." He shrugged, calm, cool, and unflappable, with naught but a telltale sparkle of roguery in his eyes.

Trinny gazed into them, the mystery of their color solved now. Dark green with shades of gray and deep blue…like cloud shadows moving over wooded hills on a warm summer day.

"So," he drawled, looking her over discreetly, "this is what you look like in the light. Not bad. I hardly recognize you without your nose all swollen."

"How now!" she retorted, yet she was grateful. His irreverent jest had instantly dispelled the awkwardness between them.

"Well, it seems we meet again," he added. "How's the ball?"

She shrugged, amused. "Same as every week."

"You're not leaving, too, are you?" he asked, glancing at the door through which her friend had gone.

"No."

"Good. I was hoping I'd run into you," he said.

"Likewise. I've been quite eager to talk to you," she said with a grin. "I have *news*."

"Hmm, so I hear. Let me escort you back to the ballroom if you're headed that way. You must tell me all." He offered her his arm as they drifted back toward the staircase. They had not been formally introduced yet, but she could not resist the invitation. The man was practically a stranger, but he was the only person on earth who knew the real truth behind her unconventional decision.

Besides, after his kiss that night, she had thought of him often. She wondered if he'd thought about her, too.

"So…it's quite the talk of the square this week. Congratulations are in order for Glendon girl number two, I understand?"

"Yes. My sister Lady Abigail and her Freddie."

"What happened?" he murmured.

"You did," she said, taking his arm when they reached the staircase. "Pardon?"

She lifted the hem of her skirts, and they proceeded up the steps.

"I decided to take your advice," she whispered. "I thought about it for two days straight, then broke the news to my parents."

"How'd they take it?" he asked in a confidential tone.

"My father was an angel. My mother was distraught. But she's better now that she gets to plan Abby's wedding."

"And your sisters?"

"Very happy."

"And most importantly, you?" he asked, studying her.

"Thrilled," she averred. "I feel as though an anchor has been lifted off my shoulders. I don't expect it will be easy, especially at first. People seem to feel sorry for me, and I hate it. But at least Lady Kirby understood."

He was shaking his head. "I can't believe you did it. Took my advice. God, I feel responsible for this!" he said as loudly as he dared.

"No, it was *good* advice!" she assured him heartily, though keeping her voice down as well. "You said to make myself happy, and that is what I've set out to do. I'm very excited about it, actually."

"Well, since it seems you changed your whole existence based on something I said off the top of my head, then I daresay we should undertake a proper introduction, if it's not too improper at this point. I am Gable Winston-McCray, Viscount Roland. And I hear you are Lady Katrina Glendon."

"My friends call me Trinny in private. You may do the same, considering the circumstances," she added meaningfully.

His slow, intimate smile needed no words to assure her he had not forgotten about the kiss.

"Well, Lady Trinny, it is very nice to meet you. And for the record, I already knew who you were, generally speaking. But I'm glad to make your acquaintance."

"Likewise, my lord."

His gaze dipped to her lips as though he, too, were remembering what they had shared.

"I trust your lady friend was happy to have her earring back," Trinny said as they continued up the stairs.

The dismissive flick of his eyebrows admitted that she was, but he looked away. "I was grateful for your help." As they reached the upper landing and walked into the ballroom, he lightly grasped her elbow. "Dance with me?"

Trinny jolted at his touch but furrowed her brow and eyed him in suspicion. "Why?"

"Er, because we're at a ball? I thought that much was obvious."

"Yes, but if this is some sort of charity demonstration—"

"My God, you say the funniest things, my fair Jupiterian or Martian or whatever you are. Are you hiding tentacles under there?" He glanced down at her skirts.

She arched a brow, and then tilted her head. "I don't want you feeling sorry for me."

"Don't be daft. I asked you to dance because I want to dance with you. Why do you always assume I have some sort of ulterior motive?"

She shrugged. "You never noticed me before."

"I didn't know you then, and now I know I'm safe with you. From the vicar's mousetrap."

"Ahh."

"To tell you the truth, it's nice to be in the company of a lady who doesn't have designs on one. Besides," he added, "you impress me."

"I do?" she asked in surprise.

"What you did takes fantastic courage, making a stand like that. It would be my honor to dance with such a woman."

She blushed a little, in spite of herself, and smiled. "Well, in that case, I accept."

He offered her his hand, she slipped her own into his, and then let him lead her toward the dance floor as the music started.

If the announcement of the second-born Glendon girl's engagement had startled Society, now the onlookers were totally confused. Everyone probably thought Lord Roland was only dancing with her out of charity, but Trinny's decision to live an independent life included no longer caring what other people thought.

This man understands me, she mused. She barely knew him, but she knew that he was on her side, and that felt wonderful.

Matchmaking mamas watched them pass in startled alarm. After all, Trinny's abandonment of the marriage game would have meant that there was one less competitor for their own daughters. So what was she doing standing up to dance with one of the most eligible—and evasive—catches in the *ton*?

Ah, well, they needn't have worried. Gable was right; she did not have designs on him. She would not have minded another kiss, to be sure, but in the main, she would much rather have a friend.

When the music started, he smiled at her and chased any last anxious thoughts right out of her head. The line of ladies curtsied, and the gentleman bowed in compliance with the dance, but Trinny had to bite her lip to keep from laughing when she spotted her sisters arrayed along the wall.

They were gaping at her.

Then her partner strode nearer and slipped his arm around her waist, and Trinny gasped in delight as he pulled her close.

# # #

Gable was fascinated to hear she had taken his advice, and privately, he reflected on how much he had thought about her kiss ever since that night. To be sure, it had preoccupied him far more than had his tryst on the same day in the same place with another woman, Lady Hayworth, of earring fame. Guilty pleasures of that sort were quickly consumed and just as quickly forgotten.

But this, now, this was something different.

He paid no attention whatsoever to the people watching them, enjoying her obvious pleasure in the dancing, and, inevitably, wondering what it would be like to bed her. He had never actually deflowered a virgin...

"So what have you been doing?" she asked cheerfully as she passed, brushing by him as the line of dancers wove about.

"The usual lot of nothing," he replied.

"Anything interesting going on in the night sky these days?"

He grinned, recalling their conversation. "Lunar eclipse coming up, according to the *Old Farmer's Almanac*," he said.

"Hmm. Isn't that an ill omen, by tradition?"

"I believe so. Could be the end of the world," he warned in a spooky tone.

"It had better not be!" she said, laughing. "I've got things I want to do!"

Gable chuckled. *I genuinely like her.* She amused him with her unexpected ways. And she was even prettier than he had thought at first, now that he could see her in the light. The kind of pretty that only grew more beautiful the more he got to know her. The soft lavender hue of her gown flattered her pale complexion and strawberry hair, and the shimmer of the chandeliers slid over the satin as it hugged her curves. He could not imagine for the life of him why she was still unattached.

She kissed well enough, God knew.

His thoughts drifted back to that bit of naughtiness. He had taken a huge risk that night, making a move like that on an unmarried young lady. But, of course, Gable liked risks, and secondly, he had wanted to show the teary-eyed little sweetheart that she in no way lacked appeal. Not to him, anyway, and he was fairly discerning.

Those tears of hers must have got to him.

Now he was all the more intrigued by her after hearing she had heeded his advice, which was always terribly flattering. In truth, he envied this freedom she had seized for herself.

As the heir to an earldom, he knew he would not have that luxury, no matter how much he might scoff at the mention of marriage.

Still, he hoped she wouldn't regret it within a fortnight. He hoped he hadn't ruined her life.

Meanwhile, some girls around the ballroom looked daggers at her, which puzzled him. Gable did not dance often, but he had the right, surely, to choose his partners as he wished. Lady Katrina was openly enjoying herself, smiling from ear to ear, her blue eyes shining with merry warmth.

He couldn't seem to peel his gaze away from her. Having watched her cry, it was good to see her happy.

"Oh dear," she murmured when she brushed past him once more as the dancers switched sides.

"What is it?" he inquired.

"Don't look now," she said confidentially, "but the cad who tossed me aside is staring at us. I daresay he's looking quite perplexed."

"For what it's worth, he's an idiot," he whispered as they circled, holding both hands.

"Well, he'd have to be, wouldn't he?" she said.

Gable's smile widened; he decided on the spot that he loved her frankness and this sense of mutual understanding he felt with her.

Very strange indeed.

But alas, when the figures of the dance turned him around again, he saw that the fool who'd rejected her wasn't the only one whose gaze was pinned on them.

So was Lord Hayworth's. Only, his was more of a murderous glare.

Gable felt his stomach clench when he noticed the older man watching his every move. Usually, Hayworth was busy leering at the debutantes and making all the young girls uncomfortable, but at the moment, Gable could practically feel the drunkard's hatred aimed at him like a spear.

Right, he thought with a slight, grim gulp, instantly aware of what was coming. *Ah, well.* Obviously, he had brought it on himself.

His cool smile wavered only for a moment as he continued dancing with the fair Katrina, saying nothing about the unpleasantness that he had a feeling was about to descend.

He scanned the ballroom briefly and noted that Lady Hayworth wasn't there. Could it be the old goat had found out and finally put his foot down with his lusty wench of a wife?

Ah, damn. Why me? Everybody had dallied with Lady Hayworth. Having hit her early forties, she was having all the fun she could cram in before her beauty faded. But it seemed that Gable was to be the lucky chap who had caught her lord and husband on the day the old drunk had had enough of her antics.

How the devil had Hayworth found out, though? Gable wondered. Had they been seen? Or had the marquess perhaps intercepted the earring when he had sent it back to her? Of course, it was possible they'd got into one of their famous rows and she had told her husband everything just to throw it in his face.

However it had happened, Gable shuddered at the whole bad business. With marriages like that all around him, was it any wonder he was in no rush to wed?

With the final bars of the music stretching out, Katrina curtsied to him, and he bowed as the song ended. He lifted her hand and kissed her knuckles through the white satin of her gloves.

"Thank you for the dance," he whispered. *"Ciao, bella."*

He tried, he really did, to get away from her before the ugliness exploded, but he failed. Hayworth wanted his blood, and came pushing toward Gable through the crowd before he'd put much distance between himself and Trinny. The instant he was in arm's reach, the marquess drew back his hand to strike Gable across the face with the traditional glove.

Gable caught his wrist in midair. "Sir—please, don't do this," he ground out in a low tone.

"What, you're a coward as well as a dishonorable cur?" the marquess slurred in red-eyed fury, then flicked a disgusted glance over him. "No accounting for taste."

Gable quirked a brow, but refrained from pointing out that Lady Hayworth *had* married *him*.

Unfortunately, the angry husband read the irreverent humor in his look and lost his mind, shoving Gable in the chest. "You find this amusing?"

Gable took a step back, catching himself. "Don't touch me, old man," he warned quietly.

"I'll kill you, is what. You are without honor, Roland! Your father should be ashamed. Name your second, and we'll settle this at dawn."

Gable glanced grimly across the crowd at Netherford. His friend gave him a regretful nod. Both of them had served in the capacity of seconds for each other before. "Netherford."

"Figures," Hayworth muttered, then spun about a trifle drunkenly and stormed off, pushing curious gawkers out of his way.

Netherford extracted himself from the knot of females surrounding him and left the room. Gable avoided the many aghast stares, but when he, too, took a step toward the exit, a hand clamped down on his arm. Still half expecting some attack, he jerked away roughly and pivoted, ready to strike.

Instead, he found Katrina.

"What was that about?" she cried, staring up at him in alarm.

Jaw clenched, Gable shook his head. "Not here."

# # #

Still in shock after what she had just witnessed, Trinny lurched into motion, hastening after Lord Roland. He strode ahead, the stunned crowd parting before him. She followed, her stomach in knots.

She did not wish to deepen this newfound scandal of his any further by involving herself, but she was panicked by the thought of him dueling. On the other hand, how much more scandalous could it get, considering who he'd chosen for his second?

Trinny spotted the dark-and-dangerous Netherford waiting for him on the landing outside the ballroom.

She caught up to Gable there herself, but got hold of him before he reached his friend. "Wait a moment, would you? Please!"

He stopped and turned to her, his chiseled face taut. "I apologize for that bit of unpleasantness, but I must bid you adieu for now, my lady."

"What just happened in there?" she exclaimed.

"I thought you saw the whole thing."

"Does this have to do with the earring?" she whispered.

Gable looked away.

Disappointment filled her. *How could you?*

She swallowed the reproachful words, but he caught the dismay in her gaze and scowled. "I don't have time for a lecture right now, so if you'll pardon me—"

"Wait. I'm not going to lecture you." She took a step closer. "Please listen, just for a moment. You gave me your advice the other night whether I wanted to hear it or not, and now I shall do the same for you. We all know this lady's reputation. Whatever mischief you got up to with her, it's not worth dying for, surely. You must apologize."

When his gaze flicked to hers, she was taken aback to find it steely. "No."

"But you're in the wrong!"

"Exactly. It would be dishonorable to grovel now and pretend I'm sorry, just because we got caught. So, no. I knew what I was doing. It was stupid, but I did it anyway. I shall delope, of course. That is apology enough."

"That doesn't mean he'll do the same. You could be killed!"

"I play for high stakes, darling. If you'll excuse me."

She huffed, at a loss, when he simply walked away, joining his friend. The two rakehells immediately headed for the stairs.

"Let me know how it goes—if you're still alive!" she called after him angrily.

He sent her a sardonic glance over his shoulder, but he made her no such promise. Trinny got the feeling his kind never did.

As he went striding off with Netherford, she stared after him, then shook her head, throwing up her hands.

I don't believe this! I finally meet a nice fellow, and he goes off to get himself killed.

On second thought, *nice* fellows didn't *get* called out to duel against outraged husbands in the first place. Just another reminder that, as smooth as he was, Lord Roland was a rakehell.

Please keep him safe, Lord. Yes, yes, I know he's a wicked sinner and doesn't deserve it, she thought, *but please…*

Surely Gable was sensible enough to swallow his pride when it came down to it. If not, she could only hope the marquess was so drunk, he'd miss.

Abigail came rushing over to her side just then. "What was all that about?" she asked breathlessly.

Distraught with worry for her wild new friend, Trinny merely shook her head.

CHAPTER 3

The Rake's Progress

*G*able watched the sunrise and wondered if it would be his last.
His palms were sweaty, but his pistol was loaded. The medic
stood by, and all that remained now was the waiting. He
refused to pace, instead standing immobile, arms folded across his chest.

It was a hell of a thing, he reflected. *Nice girls like Katrina Glendon out
there, and I'm about to die over a harlot.* He shook his head. *Bloody ridiculous.*

Well, Father had always warned him it would end like this…

The pink blush of the dawn sky glowed behind the screen of the
black trees, reminding him of Katrina's cheeks last night while they were
dancing.

He hoped Society would be kind to her. He regretted that he might
not be there to see her triumph in her own eccentric way.

Netherford came stomping over to him, disturbing his thoughts.

"This is damned unfair," the duke growled as he joined them. Their
friend Viscount Sidney followed a step behind. "We've all been with the
woman. Why did he suddenly focus in on you?"

Gable shook his head. "It doesn't matter, Jason."

"Doesn't matter?" the duke exploded. For all his faults, Netherford
was terribly loyal, at least to his male friends.

But Gable really did not wish to spend what might be his final
moments on Earth soothing the duke's fiery temper. Instead, he grasped
for his usual dry humor. "So how does the club's betting book rate my
odds?"

Sidney flashed one of his famous sunny grins, even now, and
clapped him on the shoulder. "Fifty-fifty, ol' boy. Myself, I have total

faith in you. But don't worry. If he shoots you, I have plans to do the old man a vile treachery of some kind. I'm considering all sorts of nasty options."

"Oh, I rather think vile treachery is what got me here in the first place," Gable muttered. "But thanks anyway. You're a mate."

Then Netherford was summoned to hear the instructions from the worried-looking gent acting as the neutral party.

As if they did not already know how the movements of this grim ritual played out.

"I cannot think what must've got into Lord Hayworth to start caring about his wife's indiscretions at this late date," Sidney mused aloud in a tight voice, continuing Netherford's conversation of a moment ago in an effort, Gable suspected, to distract him from thoughts of his imminent doom.

"No idea," Gable said quietly. "But I do know what got into Lady Hayworth."

Sidney snorted at his jest and offered him a flask.

"Bit early for whiskey, inn't it?" Gable said, but took it anyway. He swallowed a mouthful and handed the flask back to his friend. "Give me a moment, would you?" he murmured.

Sid nodded with a pensive smile and walked away.

Apologize... Gable found himself brooding on Katrina's advice. After all, she had taken his. *Maybe* you're *the one who should listen this time,* his brain suggested. But what was the point?

He blew out a restless exhalation and stared down at the grass, then gave in to the pacing in spite of himself.

What do I do, what do I do?

He knew he was in the wrong. And if you knew something was wrong, you ought not to do it in the first place, he reasoned, but if you did it anyway, then you had no right to try to weasel out of the consequences afterward by saying you were sorry. You took your just comeuppance like a man. That much was clear.

But was his refusal to apologize really down to honor, or was this just his pride talking?

He looked over at Lord Hayworth, who was likewise pacing back and forth on the other side of the field, a middle-aged man with his gray-haired, paunch-bellied friends around him. The lot of them could be found chasing skirts on any given night, as though they were still Gable's age—under thirty, instead of over sixty.

Is that how we end up, too? he wondered. *Netherford and Sidney and me and all the rest?*

Because if that was his fate, Gable wasn't sure he really cared about surviving today. It all seemed so petty and pointless.

"Nothing new to report," Netherford said as he returned, his dark, fiery eyes looking even blacker than usual. "Twenty paces, fire at the same time, as you requested, rather than by turns. Let's get this over with, shall we?"

Gable looked at his friend for a moment.

"Tell Hayworth I want to talk to him first," he said abruptly.

Both his fellow rakehells turned to him in surprise, but Netherford nodded and went to convey his request to the enemy.

Gable drummed his fingers on his arm as he waited for another moment, and then walked through the wet grass to the center of the field for a brief parlay with the old man he had callously wronged.

Sid and Netherford followed. The marquess's friends trailed him as well.

And so, with their seconds hovering nearby, Gable met Lord Hayworth in the middle of the field.

As he scanned the marquess's hard, lined face, he noted the scruff of the man's salt-and-pepper beard. Hayworth looked a bit more sober than he had last night in the ballroom, but his eyes were still bloodshot.

He's the one who should be worried, Gable thought. *I'm younger, I'm stronger, I've got excellent eyesight. My hands are much steadier than his, and I'm a damned good shot. Besides, his wife was the one who wanted me. The whole damned thing was her idea. I just went along with it.*

Then a startling thought slid through his mind out of nowhere. *Maybe he's trying to kill himself.*

I might, too, if I were in his shoes. Made a laughingstock like that…

"Well? What do you want?" Hayworth demanded in a gruff tone.

Gable dropped his gaze as a wave of pity washed through him. He cleared his throat. "My lord: I wish to offer you my deepest apologies for what took place," he said in a clipped, formal tone.

Hayworth's eyebrow arched high.

"It was, er, a moment of weakness for which I am truly sorry."

The still-intoxicated marquess studied him with wary disdain. "Well, that's new. But it changes nothing. I'm still goin' to kill you."

"Weren't you listening?" Sid exclaimed from a few feet behind him. "He just apologized, damn you! Don't be daft. Call it off! There is no need for bloodshed here!"

"Take the chance you've been given," Netherford chimed in. "Besides, it isn't as though *you* never did the same when you were our age!"

"Aye, he still does!" Sid agreed.

But their contributions only made the marquess angrier. "You two can keep your damned opinions to yourselves! I know you've all been with her—and I'm sick of it. I've had enough."

"At least we don't go around groping virgins like you do," Netherford said under his breath.

"Well," Sidney amended, glancing wryly at the duke.

His little jest was well timed.

Indeed, it was said Lord Sidney could charm the very birds from the trees, and he offered Hayworth a penitent smile, looking like a choirboy.

"I'm sure there's plenty of blame to go around here, my lord. But come, sir," the golden-haired viscount cajoled the old man, "Roland said he was sorry. We will all stay away from her in future—you have our word. You don't really want to do this. What will you say to the lad's father?"

Hayworth turned his bleary stare from Sidney to Gable once more. He narrowed his eyes, sizing him up, but then he shook his head. "Roland brought this on himself. It's time that one of you sons o' bitches got what you deserve," he grumbled, and walked toward his side of the field.

"Bloody *hell*," Netherford muttered.

"Your neck aside, Roland, I must say I'm a bit worried about his wife," Sidney said as they all retreated to their respective areas. "She could be in real danger."

"Or already dead," Netherford added in a low tone.

Sidney nodded. "We'll go there after this to check on her."

"Provided all goes well." Netherford gazed at Gable for a moment. "Is there anything else you need?"

Gable wanted to ask his friends to tell his father he was sorry if he fell, but his voice had left him. He just shook his head.

"Well, good luck, then," the duke said.

Sid clapped Gable on the shoulder, then the two retreated from the field.

Time began to move with dreamlike fluidity with the nearness of death. The moments smeared together while the morning's birdsong thundered in his ears, a deafening cacophony.

Gun in hand, Gable went to stand in the center of the field back to back with the aging rakehell. He could smell the sour liquor fumes pouring off the old man.

"Can I just ask you one question?" he inquired without looking over his shoulder.

"Go ahead," Hayworth grunted.

"Why me? Why now?"

He paused. "Because she promised me last month that she would stop. And I believed her."

Gable winced, sinking even deeper into guilty self-recrimination. "I didn't know you were trying to make it better between the two of you."

"Would it have mattered?" Hayworth asked in bitter quiet.

"Of course it would've mattered!" Gable whispered. "I thought it was...business as usual!"

Hayworth's only answer was a low, disgusted growl.

"Gentlemen! Proceed," came the order.

They parted.

Pistol upright in his grasp, his heart hammering with sickening force, his mates staring from the sides of the field in dismay—and Lady Katrina Glendon probably off praying for him somewhere—Gable walked, counting off the paces.

Nine, ten, eleven...

I can't die now. Not for this. I've never even been in love.

A ray of light broke through the forest and sliced a golden line down the middle of the field. He walked through it.

Sixteen, seventeen, eighteen...

His senses sharpened to a fine point.

So be it. If this was to be his fate, he had no one else to blame.

His finger curled around the trigger, every impulse in him screaming with the instinct for self-defense, but Gable wouldn't do it.

Nineteen...

Twenty.

He stopped, pivoted, and fired at the sky, not even taking aim. The shot roared, the flash leaped, the smoke puffed from the barrel of his pistol. He shut his eyes and braced for the bullet, but instead of slamming into his body, it tore across the fleshy muscle of his arm.

It burned like hell. His body jerked away from the pain automatically, and a curse escaped him. But when he flicked his eyes open, he saw Hayworth standing in the morning light with a look of satisfied reproach.

The medic came running, as did his friends. Gable returned the old man's stare with gratitude—and pity—well aware that he had just been intentionally spared.

But only because he had apologized.

With blood pouring out of his arm, he was dazed to realize that Katrina's advice had just saved his life.

# # #

Gable was not surprised in the least to receive his father's summons later that morning.

After the medic had bandaged his arm, he had gone home to his terrace house in Moonlight Square while his friends went to make sure Lady Hayworth hadn't been murdered.

He ate a slice of toast and drank some tea, which was all his knotted stomach could handle after that ordeal, but the light breakfast helped restore a sense of normality. After this, he went up to his chamber to strip off his bloodied shirt, clean himself up, and get some much-needed sleep.

At that point, he had been awake for nearly twenty-four hours. He could have fallen asleep immediately, but the moment he closed his eyes, his brain offered up the image of Lady Katrina Glendon staring up at him in wide-eyed worry, just as she had looked when they had last parted in the ballroom.

He had to let her know he was still alive, since, for whatever reason, she seemed to care. Arm throbbing, he heaved himself out of bed, his whole body feeling leaden now that his heightened state of alert from the duel was wearing off. He ambled across to his dressing table, which also served as an informal writing desk. There, he dipped his quill pen in the inkpot and penned her a short note.

Dear Lady Katrina, he started, then stopped with a frown.

No. That felt too stodgy, he thought, considering how familiar she already felt to him, even though he had only twice been in her company. Somehow, she had already taken on the halo of a closer sort of friend to him than that.

He crumpled up the first piece of paper and threw it aside. Sliding another toward himself, he tried again, this time opting for his own blunt style of simplicity.

Alive. Huzzah.

He drew a funny little face of some sort at the bottom and signed off, *Roland.*

Postscript: Thanks for your concern.

He sent the message off with his footman, then tumbled into bed and could've slept all day, but, alas, his servants woke him only two hours later, and there was only one motive that could cause them to do such a thing: a message from his sire.

He would really have preferred a note in answer from Lady Katrina. But the Earl of Sefton's terse wording—*Your presence is requested at your earliest convenience*—was better translated from Fatherese as: *Get your arse over here now, you worthless wastrel.*

There were some forces of nature that not even a duel-fighting rakehell dared defy. Not when his sire controlled the family purse strings.

Gable breathed a curse, wiped the sleep out of his eyes, and snapped to it.

He had to wear a roomier tailcoat than usual to accommodate the bandage wrapped around his bicep. His arm burned like hell, and he was a little pale from lack of sleep, and probably from blood loss.

But other than that, by the time he strode into his father's grand mansion in St. James's, he looked more or less normal.

The old family servants smiled fondly at him as they ushered him toward his waiting father's study, and the butler offered a discreet look of sympathy as he led him thence.

Admittedly, Gable's heart pounded as he approached the door. The march to his place of punishment was not unfamiliar, but it had been a long time—years—since he had been officially called on the carpet.

The trim, gray-haired butler, Hawkins, went in ahead of him to make sure His Lordship was ready to receive Gable.

Then he was ushered in to account for his actions. Hawkins whisked away, leaving him standing at attention across from his sire.

"Ahem. Good morning, Father. You wished to see me, sir?"

The Earl of Sefton was about Lord Hayworth's age but his opposite in temperament. He stood by the window, gazing out at the birds in the garden. His only hobbies were golf and a bit of bird-watching.

Dull fellow, wrapped up in his parliamentary work, Gable reflected, still waiting for any sort of response.

But he knew the earl was choosing how to begin, likely debating with himself as he stood in the morning light, cravat perfectly starched, posture ramrod straight, hair thinning, but not a one out of place.

"I trust you are unscathed?" At last, His Lordship pivoted with his usual automaton-like stiffness.

Gable braced himself and stood at attention. Actually, he had been shot in the arm, but he was alive, and any such complaints would have been duly met with the frostiest scorn. "Yes, sir."

The earl's patrician face was expressionless, but his eyes were fiery. "I hear you have been busy, sir," he said politely, simmering anger just beneath the surface.

It would soon erupt, Gable had no doubt. He kept his mouth shut and let his father have his rant.

"You do realize you are, first, a grown man, not a boy, and second, the heir to an earldom, yes?"

Gable tensed. "Er, yes, sir. On both counts."

"Good. That is very good, son." Radiating righteous indignation, his father lifted his chin and attempted to look down his nose at him. But he could not really do that anymore, now that Gable was taller than he was. "You further realize that if you die, our title goes to a very obnoxious branch of the family?"

"Of course I do. If I could just say "

"I hear you deloped," Father interrupted. "And even…apologized?"

Silenced, Gable merely nodded.

"Well. That much, at least, shows honor." Lord Sefton paced around his desk. "And that is the only reason I am not cutting you off immediately."

Gable looked at him in alarm.

The earl sighed. "I am extremely tired of your immaturity, Lord Roland. It ends now, do you understand me? Netherford is a terrible influence on you," he added. "Stay away from him."

Gable gritted his teeth. Ah, but he was used to this. Being under his father's control. He chafed at it with every fiber of his being. "As you said, sir, I am a grown man. I'm sure I can choose my own friends."

When his father let this go with no more than a disapproving glance, Gable got his first uneasy inkling that the earl had something larger in mind.

"Very well. But I have made a decision regarding your affairs."

"Oh, really?"

"Since you are so keen to sample other men's wives, I think it's time you had one of your own."

"Pardon?" Gable blurted out.

"I am giving you exactly four weeks from today to find a suitable girl and marry her. You have until Saturday, sixth of June. If you fail to do this thing—if you refuse—then you shall live in penury, for that is also the day that, if you fail, I shall be cutting off your funds. My decision is final. This matter is not open for discussion. Let me know when you find her. Good day, sir."

Gable flinched, but he was hardly surprised. "Father, I don't think you understand. If I could just explain—"

"No, Gable, *you* don't understand!" his father suddenly thundered at him, the impassioned use of his first name betraying the fact that he was not just angry, but frightened, belatedly, at how things could have gone. "You are my son! You could have been killed. And even if you weren't, *you* could have killed a man this morning! Do you really want to live with such a burden on your soul, all for the sake of your mindless pleasures? Truly, have I sired a conscienceless fool?"

His father marched closer. "Did it never occur to you, in addition, that dueling is illegal in the first place? Is my son, a future peer, to be arrested for breaking the law like a common criminal? Do you have any idea what it would do to my bill in Parliament, the one I have been working on for the past two years, Gable?

"And even if you aren't arrested," he charged on, not letting Gable get a word in edgewise, "since justice so often turns a blind eye to our kind, people learn about these things! How does this make you look to decent folk? Adultery and dueling?" he cried. "What sort of example, I ask, are you setting for the lower orders?"

"I never set myself up to be an example for the lower orders, Father," Gable attempted angrily, but his father talked over him.

"Well! If hitting you in the purse strings is the only way to get your attention, then you leave me no choice. I did not want it to come to this, but I would be remiss in my duties as your parent if I let this continue." The earl rounded his great oaken desk again, resuming his seat of authority and power. "If you wish to keep your handsome house in Moonlight Square, dear boy, your memberships at the Grand Albion and White's; if you wish your bills paid to the tailor and the boot maker, and the pubs and the brothels, and the wages of your household staff paid, then you will do your duty and comply. Any questions?"

Why, it was the most his father had spoken to him in years.

Gable dropped his gaze, but could not quite hold his tongue. He lifted his chin, politely glaring. "Why don't you just choose my wife for me, as well, Father? I'm sure you must have ideas about that. You always seem to know what would be best."

"Don't give me your cheek," the earl warned. "No. So long as she is suitable, you will choose your own bride. Perhaps, then, you might just be inspired to be a faithful husband after having tempted so many other men's wives astray. I expect a report on your progress within a sennight. However, ahem, as it happens, I did make a list of my preferences for you," he admitted. "Here. You may peruse them at your leisure."

He slid a piece of paper across his desk to Gable, who picked it up, numb.

"If you wish information on the young ladies or their families, that can be arranged."

In shock, Gable skimmed the list, so incredulous he almost could have laughed. "These are the daughters of your political allies!"

A defensive flicker passed behind his father's eyes, but he shrugged. "So? Strengthening such ties would be most advantageous. Well, you might as well go and have a look at them. It can't hurt!"

Jaw clenched, Gable refused to read any further. It was all he could do not to tear the paper into shreds. Furious, he felt as though a noose were closing around his neck, even as he'd barely just survived a duel. His father, the political lords, and their simpering daughters could all go hang.

His pulse thumped. "Will there be anything else, sir?" he asked through gritted teeth.

"Why, yes, in fact, there is. And this part may please you. I am not so cruel a father as to know how difficult this may be for you. So I have devised a couple of carrots, as well as the stick, for my wayward son," he said dryly. "Choose a bride off *my* list, and I will give you Castle McCray for your country house. You always liked it up there in Scotland, by the sea. Furthermore, should you produce a child within a year of your marriage, I will double your monthly allowance."

Gable stared at him in amazement. "You think you can bribe me into having a child, too?"

"When you have a family, your financial needs will increase," his father said in an oh-so-reasonable tone.

And although this was quite true, and very much the way things were done, Gable was revolted. Dazed, he folded up the list and tucked it into the breast pocket of his waistcoat, feeling like some sort of stud horse about to be crossbred with some equally purebred filly, for no other bloody reason than to produce the wanted foal.

It was repulsive, he thought, standing there while his father stared matter-of-factly at him, waiting for him to absorb his instructions.

Alas, his reaction was probably not what His Lordship had desired. For Gable was suddenly filled with rebellion, glad for every woman he had seduced. In that moment, he was a rakehell to the core, worse even than Netherford—defiantly proud of his charity work in giving Society's poor, hobbled broodmares a brief, wild taste of freedom. Hell, every one of them deserved it after being auctioned off, as was the way of their class, and put through this exercise in humiliation.

He could barely wait to pleasure even more of them. He almost told his father to take his fortune and shove it up his arse, but he bit back the words at the last minute...for he liked his easy life, and had no desire to acquaint himself with the sponging house.

Then he was disgusted with himself. God, maybe he really was a whore.

At a loss, Gable just shook his head, turned away, and walked toward the door without even bidding his elder a good day.

"Are you quite clear on what is expected of you?" the earl clipped out after him.

"Crystal," he muttered, and slammed the door behind him.

His heart was pounding and his mind was a blur as he gusted out of the house in a fury, marching down the pavement, ignoring passersby.

With the powerless sense of rage washing through him, he could suddenly relate all the more to the marital pressure that had driven Lady Katrina to angry, futile tears on the night he had met her.

The thought of her stopped him mid-stride.

Hold on!

He took his father's list out and unfolded it, a crafty smile spreading across his face. *Well, I'll be damned.* There it was, third name down, in his father's own hand: *Earl of Beresford — several eligible daughters, your choice.*

"Oh, ho, ho…" A vengeful snicker escaped him. Now, here was one solution he could live with.

Hell, I can even get a castle out of the deal.

For he knew one *very* agreeable daughter of Lord Beresford who'd likely be glad for any offer she could get at this point. Relief flooded him. *Thank God.* Their meeting at the gazebo that night must've been fate.

Lady Katrina was the obvious solution. He liked her, and he was more than willing to bed her.

Repeatedly.

They got on well enough, and she already knew he had no serious intention of ever changing his picaresque ways, especially now that his controlling father was trying to force him to do so. Two birds, one stone.

Gable could be very stubborn indeed.

Well, Trinny, my girl, he thought roguishly, jumping up into his phaeton and feeling quite pleased with himself. *I hope you like Scotland.*

Of course, he knew full well that she already liked *him.* Why, he might even fancy getting the chance to play her rescuer, saving her from her spinsterhood fate.

A good deed, after all his wicked ones.

It never crossed his mind that her answer could ever be anything other than a joyful yes.

CHAPTER 4

A Dubious Proposal

*O*ne of the most wonderful and unexpected consequences that dawned on Trinny after choosing the single life was that, at last, she could eat anything she wanted.

The prospect of flouting Mama's longstanding order to curb her hunger for the sake of a trim figure filled her with wicked glee. Now free from the oppressive obligation of snaring a husband, she decided to indulge that very day.

After all, she had cause to celebrate. Dear Lord Sweet Cheeks had survived his duel.

And so, she ended her daily constitutional in Hyde Park by going straight to the famous sweets shop, Gunter's, with her lady's maid in tow. With a smile from ear to ear, Trinny waited in the queue, discussing the confections on offer with her maid with childlike excitement. When she reached the front counter, she ordered a dainty goblet of chocolate ice cream with a great, shameless dollop of whipped cream on top. She bought some for her maid, too.

"Oh, miss, it's not necessary," Cora protested.

"Eat, girl! Lord knows you deserve it for all the work you do keeping me and all my sisters looking coiffed and well-dressed. Besides, you're too skinny. What flavor?"

Cora could not mask her grin, and said, "Pistachio."

Then they walked back out into the midday sunshine of Berkeley Square, and Trinny couldn't help but gloat at all the starving debutantes who foolishly felt sorry for her. She and her maid drifted down the pavement with their treats, in raptures.

"Mmm." Trinny ate the ice cream luxuriously, licking bite after bite off the little spoon, making sounds of pleasure at the sheer deliciousness of it.

She only realized that perhaps some might think she was making a pig of herself when a smooth voice drawled, "So, it's good, then?"

She looked up from her creamy, sugary treat and suddenly found herself face to face with Lord Roland.

His deep green eyes danced as he watched her gulp the mouthful down in embarrassment.

Blushing, she laughed and dabbed at her mouth with the napkin provided by the shop. "You're not going to ask me to share it, are you?"

"Aw." He feigned a pout, then narrowed his eyes. "Hand it over."

She turned away, pretending to hoard it, but when he grinned, she laughed again and gave him the goblet and spoon. He proceeded to take a huge bite.

"Greedy! Leave me some!" she scolded playfully.

He surrendered it back to her, his mouth full, but his glance merry.

She hugged the treat close to tease him, enjoying their camaraderie.

"So," she said at length, "you're alive."

He nodded but did not answer aloud, still quieted by the ice cream in his mouth.

"I was so relieved to get your note. Thank you for remembering to send it," she added. "How did it go?"

He shrugged, still eating, but gestured in the direction of Moonlight Square, and then he walked with her. Cora chaperoned, following them at a respectful distance. Fortunately, the environs of Gunter's were considered a perfectly respectable place for young ladies to be seen in the company of gentlemen. For that reason, Trinny did not intend to go far. Besides, they had to return their goblets and utensils.

"Thank God you didn't get shot," Trinny said.

"Actually, I did," he informed her after he finally swallowed.

"What?" she cried, turning to scan him. "Where?"

"Across the arm. Don't worry, it was just a scratch."

"Oh, you poor thing! Here. Clearly you need this more than I do." She gave him back the ice cream.

He took it without argument. "If you ask me, I got off easy," he mumbled, then scooped another spoonful from the glass goblet. "Well done, by the way. The chocolate is the best."

"Does it hurt?" she asked. "Oh, never mind—silly question."

He chuckled. "It stung."

"Well, I hope you learned your lesson!" she chided, nudging him with her elbow as he ate his next bite.

"About that…"

She furrowed her brow and looked askance at him.

"It's been an interesting morning." He licked his lips and handed her back her ice cream. "My father heard about the duel and summoned me for a lecture."

"Oh dear." She gave him a sympathetic frown. "One can't really blame him for being angry, though."

"True," Lord Roland agreed. Then he paused, studying the pavement as they strolled along.

"So what did he say?" she asked.

He slid his hands into his pockets with a shrug. "He ordered me to marry or have my funds cut off."

"Oh, that is harsh! You must be hating this," she offered in heartfelt concern. "Based on what you said at the gazebo, I know marriage was the last thing you wanted."

"Well, he is going to force my compliance. He even gave me a list."

"A list?" she echoed.

"Of approved young ladies."

She shook her head. "How very helpful of him."

His gaze slid sideways cautiously to her. "You were on it."

"What?" She stopped in her tracks and stared at him. "Me?"

"Apparently your father is one of his political allies. So?" He gave her a beguiling little smile. "What do you think?"

Trinny stared up at him, incredulous. "I'm sorry, are…are you asking me…?"

"To be my wife, yes." His expression was unreadable, as though he were at the gambling table. Not a flicker of doubt passed behind his eyes. His gaze was steady. "I do see the irony, of course, considering I was the one who told you to shun the vicar's mousetrap. But you and I seem to get on rather well, and considering the circumstances… Well, I don't think we'd do too badly, leg-shackled together. So what do you say?"

She was quite speechless for a moment.

"Oh dear," he murmured at her continued silence. "Well, say *something*."

"*Now* you ask me?" She shook her head, at a loss, then snorted. "You have some timing, my lord."

He furrowed his brow, worriedly searching her face, as though this was not quite the reaction he'd expected.

"The timing was not of my own choosing," he reminded her as they walked on.

"I daresay! If it was of your own choosing, you wouldn't be here at all."

He did her the courtesy, at least, of not denying it, but conceded this with an uncertain shrug.

"Lord Roland—"

"Gable," he corrected her.

"I just finished taking your advice!"

"I know, I know." He sighed.

"I changed my whole life based on what you said to me—because you inspired me! I gave my parents this whole big dramatic speech! I've already brazened out Society's reaction! If I go back on my decision now, the whole *ton* is going to think it was just a sorry lie on my part, and that you were forced into it, and only chose me out of pity!"

Which was exactly the case, she realized, the thought instantly curdling the ice cream in her belly.

But meanwhile, her handsome companion was scoffing at her words as they resumed their walk, Trinny moving dazedly.

"That's not the case. I like you well, my lady. I find you very agreeable, and I think you know that's the truth."

She eyed him in suspicion, then paused to ask Cora to take her empty goblet and spoon back to the shop for her. She did not want the servant overhearing any more of their conversation.

"It makes sense to me," he said.

"A marriage of convenience."

"Yes."

"But you said marriage is a cage, a trap. And I assume—forgive me if I'm wrong—that you have no desire to, er, shall we say, change your ways?"

He avoided her gaze, but his diplomatic silence told her all she needed to know.

She shook her head, realizing the firm conditions of his offer. *What nerve!* This was not a marriage proposal; it was a rooming arrangement.

"No, thanks. I'll not be made a laughingstock over a cheating husband," she said, then shuddered. "No, thank you, indeed."

"Oh come," he cajoled her, "it'll be fun."

She eyed him in severe disapproval. No doubt that charm usually got the rogue everything he wanted, especially where females were concerned.

"You realize we only just met? We barely know each other," she pointed out.

"That is not uncommon among those betrothed, as I'm sure you are aware."

She scowled at him, ignoring the bizarre reality that after being rejected by far less desirable suitors, she couldn't seem to get rid of this one.

"You don't want to be a countess?" he goaded her, as though his vanity had taken hold now. Like he had to win this contest for his pride's sake.

Why? Because to be rejected by the girl no one else wanted was just too much? She gave him a dirty look.

"Well, at least it must mean something to you that I don't care if you're a quiz—your words, not mine!" he reminded her when she belted him in the arm for that remark. "Ow! Do you mind? Bullet wound."

"You deserve it," she muttered.

"Now, now, dear girl," he soothed, eyeing her in bemused fascination. "I understand that the, er, limits on what I'm offering you may not be entirely to your liking—"

"But beggars can't be choosers? Is that it? I thought you applauded my decision!"

"That is *not* what I was going to say! I was going to say that at least I accept you for who you are. You don't have to pretend with me or ever feel nervous, the way you described feeling around those other chaps. Ever since that night I found you crying in the park... Well, I happen to like you being eccentric. That must count for something!"

"Certainly." She gazed up at him in dismay, tempted, in light of everything. *Don't do it*, her heart warned. *It can only lead to disaster.* She swallowed hard and shook her head. "Your acceptance of me as I am makes me very glad to have you for a *friend*, Lord Roland."

His eyes widened, as though no female had ever said such a thing to him before.

Cora returned and they walked on, resuming their slow trek homeward to Moonlight Square. It wasn't far.

"Dear me, a friend!" he echoed in astonishment at last, his air of sardonic humor beginning to run a bit thin, by the sound of it.

"I'm sorry," she offered.

He seemed to struggle for words. "I confess I am amazed, my lady. Am I to understand you are really turning me down?"

"You're the one who told me not to marry."

"Well, I've changed my mind!" he said with a flash of annoyance. "And maybe this time, it's you who needs to swallow your pride."

"Me?"

"Come, reconsider."

"There are other names on your father's list, surely. Try *them*."

"I don't want them. I like you. You make me laugh. There's a castle in it for you," he added with a roguish glance.

"What castle?" she mumbled, admittedly intrigued and already beginning to wonder if she was an idiot for balking.

"Castle McCray. It came into my family's possession through the Scottish clan McCray, our ancestors. I love that place," he added. "It's become our hunting lodge, up in Galloway. Wonderful seaside retreat in the summers. My father says I can have it if I pick one of his girls. I'll share it with you gladly," he teased, nudging her with his elbow.

She looked askance at him, then shook her head. Did he really think a bribe would sway her?

"My dear Lord Roland, you really are a piece of work."

"I said call me Gable," he insisted in a droll tone. "I don't deem it too improper, since, after all, I am your future husband."

"No, you're not," she countered sweetly.

"Yes, I am," he assured her in a tone just as mild.

"Go away!" she said, laughing despite her vexation when they reached the corner of Moonlight Square.

He stopped and turned to study her for a moment.

"What?" she asked, growing self-conscious. When he didn't answer, she hesitated. "You're angry at me," she said.

"No. Just surprised. When you chose to embrace spinsterhood, I guess I didn't think you entirely meant it."

Trinny gazed at him, unsure, herself, all of a sudden—and cursing him for making her so. What was wrong with her?

"I mean, you must be curious," he murmured, leaning closer.

"About what?"

He flicked a smoky glance over her. "The marriage bed."

Her eyes widened, and a red-hot blush flamed into her cheeks. "You did *not* really just say that to me?"

"You're missing out," he taunted softly. "Especially with me."

Her jaw dropped. "You coxcomb," she uttered.

He shrugged and sauntered away. "Ask anyone."

"That's p-precisely the problem!" she sputtered.

But the expert seducer merely sent her a smile. "Do let me know if you change your mind," he said politely as he took his leave of her, ambling off in the direction of his own house as they reached Moonlight Square. "But don't dawdle, my sweet. Father only gave me four weeks to secure a bride."

"You let me know if *you* change your mind!" she shot back, her face still hot.

He furrowed his brow at her in question.

"About your wicked ways!"

"Ah, that." But the frank look he gave her required no words to tell her, with unmistakable eloquence, that the other girls on his father's list weren't going to care about his peccadilloes.

"Stop," she ordered.

He stopped. "You're very stubborn," he said. "You could be the next Countess of Sefton. With a castle and several fine estates. And a damned fine husband, if I say so myself."

"Gable," she said softly, tentatively, trying out his Christian name. Not because he'd ever be her husband. But because she truly *had* come to consider him a particular friend after his advice had altered the course of her entire life. "I won't be changing my mind."

He considered this, the mask of suave humor finally melting away. "Why not? Am I so bad?"

"I don't want to be the one who cages you. Not now that we've become friends. You told me the truth of your opinion on marriage the night we met. So it's no use. And besides…" Her words trailed off.

"Besides what?" he asked quietly.

"I don't want *you* to be the one who really breaks my heart. Because you could."

Her heart thundered at her own stark admission.

He tilted his head and gazed at her for a long moment from where he stood a few feet away. Then he returned, lifted her hand gently from her side, and kissed her knuckles.

"Then I retract my offer, sweet Katrina. Because I fear you're probably right, and I would not hurt you for all the castles in the Realm. Farewell for now, my lovely friend," he added softly, and, releasing her hand, he turned around and strolled away.

And, Trinny feared, likely took her heart with him.

# # #

Gable walked away with the taste of ice cream on his tongue and the sting of rejection smarting worse than the pain in his arm.

He could not believe the little quiz had turned him down. *But so be it.*

Startled, confused, with his pride bruised, and yet intrigued, he could feel her gaze on his back as he cut through the park, heading for his side of Moonlight Square.

Well, damn, he thought with a droll wince, *maybe I'm not quite the catch I thought.*

But no matter. He did not want to marry someone who didn't want to marry him. More importantly, she was right, and Gable did not trust himself enough not to hurt her.

One of the other young ladies on his father's list would no doubt do just as well. They'd probably give him less trouble, too.

For the next week, he went down his father's list, ticking off the possible brides suggested to him. He sought them out from a wary distance at social events, had a look, made a few discreet inquiries about them. Asked his father for details. But none of them raised much enthusiasm in him.

Lady Simone Pelletier was quite young and still seemed afraid of her own shadow in Society. No, too shy. He did not want a wife too terrified of his attention to have a conversation with him.

Lady Hypatia Fox was a scandal waiting to happen. A loud, dashing girl who loved to hunt, and surrounded herself with equally loud, fun-loving fellows from the sporting set. She had a marvelous reputation as a fearless rider. But Gable was not interested in snaring the girl who fancied herself one of the boys. That was just plain trouble.

Miss Adora Walker was as beautiful as an angel, literally. A once-in-a-decade sort of beauty. She was young, too, but Gable was entranced enough by her exquisite face to seek an introduction. When he talked to her, though, good God, he could not flee fast enough. She was fantastically proud of her own righteous virtue, and nothing was worth having to live with that. What God had added to her in beauty, He must have subtracted from any vestige of a sense of humor.

The last girl had a horse face to go with her huge dowry, but when he saw her digging a finger into her ear and then studying whatever she had found in there, he gagged a bit and turned away.

Thus, the riches of his father's bride list too soon ran out.

Growing desperate, he expanded his angry and disgusted search. This would not get him the castle, but at least he wouldn't be cut off.

There were other nice girls who seemed appealing once he started really looking. The vibrant, raven-haired beauty, Lady Serena Parker, oozed sensuality, but he found out she was all but betrothed. Gable wondered if he could steal her from her beau, some bookish, bespectacled fop who rambled on about his literary project collecting old folklore and putting the tales in a tome. He'd probably be doing the vibrant beauty a favor, saving her from such a dull fellow, and a younger son, to boot, but he decided not to meddle, and pressed on in the hunt.

Next he considered Miss Felicity Carvel, a slim, stately blonde with a reserved demeanor that pleased him. A niece of the Marquess of Bellingham, she had excellent breeding, and everything about her seemed impeccable. She was kind, too, obviously devoted to caring for the old dragon, Lady Kirby, her great-aunt, whom she had served as companion ever since her own mother died.

Perfect wife material, Gable had to admit.

But to his surprise, his friend Netherford sent him the strangest look while Gable was dancing with Miss Carvel. Something along the lines of a brief, deadly glare.

Right. Well, then. No Miss Carvel for him. Gable had thanked her for the dance and backed away. Something was definitely afoot between the duke and the sister of Netherford's boyhood friend, Major Pete Carvel. What that might be, Gable was too polite to ask, but he had no intention of poaching on his fellow rakehell's territory.

Besides, the truth was, the longer he stayed away from Katrina, the more he grew obsessed with seeing her again.

He craved her company, he knew not why. He kept wondering what she was doing, what hilariously odd thing she might say the next time he talked to her. Since his campaign for a bride was such a dismal failure so far, perhaps she'd have some advice for him on how to proceed.

Then it dawned on Gable he had never even told her that he'd taken her advice in the duel. He supposed he hadn't mentioned it the last time he'd seen her because it had needled his pride to admit he had apologized after specifically saying he would not.

In hindsight, however, she really did deserve to know, since, after all, she had taken *his* advice.

Indeed, his *wonderful* advice was the very thing causing him all these bridal headaches now. *And well done on that,* he sarcastically congratulated himself.

He'd call on her tomorrow, he decided as he lay awake in bed that night alone.

Having devised this excuse to visit his "friend" again, he finally fell asleep, only to ravish her in a scarlet dream of unbridled sex that shocked him awake after midnight, panting, sweat-soaked, and hard.

Oh damn, he thought, trembling, as he finally reached the grim realization that something serious was happening to him where she was concerned.

He pushed those dangerous thoughts away and lay back down, but he couldn't fall asleep again.

# # #

It was midmorning when he crossed Moonlight Square to call on her.

The maid who had been with her on the day he'd shared Katrina's ice cream answered the door and told him the lady was out in the garden.

"Just go through the passage, sir," she instructed, and while he did so, walking down the shady path between the elegant townhouses to knock on the quaint garden gate, the maid rushed out there, as well, playing chaperone again.

Thankfully, the lady's maid was unobtrusive—unlike the several heads of Katrina's younger sisters furtively peering out the window above, trying to spy on them.

"Hullo, neighbor," he greeted her, his heart lifting at the sight of her tending a yellow-flowered bush of Scotch broom, garden snippers in hand. A wide-brimmed straw hat protected her face from the sun, and the gauzy ends of the flowered scarf tied around its crown billowed in the light morning breeze.

His gaze moved softly over her. She was as pretty as the primroses blooming in the border by her feet, but Gable did not say so. He did not wish to seem like some idiotic lovelorn swain as he leaned his elbows casually atop the waist-high gate.

"Why, hullo there!" she called back brightly. "Oh, come in, come in! You don't have to stand out there!"

She rose from her knees, dusted off the apron she wore over her skirts, and came toward him with a broad smile. He accepted the invitation, letting himself into the family's small but pleasant garden.

She propped her hands on her waist as he walked toward her. "What are you doing here?" she asked with a jaunty air, reaching down to snap a dead bloom off a red geranium in an urn nearby.

"Does a friend really need a reason to call?" he countered, still amused and yet wincing over that "friend" speech she had given him.

Usually, he was the one offering up such sentiments. It worked well as an apologetic *cheerio* to overzealous lovers of whom he had tired, or to those who were becoming too attached.

The funny thing was, Katrina had actually meant the words just the way she had said them. He liked that about her. She was frank and unpretentious. But there was one mystery… How was it that she seemed to grow more beautiful every time they met?

"So what's all this, then?" he inquired to get the conversation going, since, admittedly, there was a little awkwardness between them.

She glanced around at the garden. "It's such a fine day, I thought I would do little puttering out here."

He smiled. "Having fun?"

"Loads. I'm taking a break from wedding duties. It's a madhouse in there." When she glanced toward her house, she must have caught sight of her sisters eavesdropping, for she frowned at the window.

When Gable glanced up, the little heads had disappeared.

Katrina shook off her obvious vexation at the spies and looked back at him. "We've been working round the clock on wedding business," she said. "My sisters and I have been writing our fingers off with the invitations. You'll receive one, too."

He furrowed his brow. "I don't even know your sister."

"Ahem, but my father and yours are political allies, remember?" she asked pertly.

He snorted. "Right. How could I forget?"

She shrugged. "A wedding is political in some ways."

He gave her a long-suffering look. "You have just described my entire week."

She flashed a smile and gestured at the pleasant wooden bench under a trellis dripping with purple blooms of wisteria. "Shall we sit?"

They did, while her maid took up her prim post on the backstairs across the garden from them, keeping them discreetly in view.

She needn't have worried; Gable was on his best behavior. He flipped the tails of his light brown coat out behind him and sat down beside Katrina.

"Did I mention I'm to be the maid of honor?" she remarked as she drew off her thick gardening gloves.

He looked askance at her. "Does that bother you?"

"No. Why would it? Oh…because of my own status?" She paused, mulling the question, then shrugged. "I suppose it hurts a little. But I'm not letting it bother me. It's my sister's happiness that counts. She and her intended are very much in love. As it should be," she added with a meaningful glance.

Gable just looked at her.

"Well? How goes the search?"

He let out a sigh. "Abysmal. Have you by chance changed your mind yet?"

"You retracted the offer, remember? To protect me from your wicked ways."

"I'll retract my retraction."

"You're still wicked, though."

"Depends on who you compare me to." He stretched his legs out before him and looked at his boots. "This isn't very nice of you, you know. I accept *you* for who you are. Why can't you do the same for me? I still think it would work out quite nicely for us, if you could."

"Ah, I see. That way, you get everything you want, while I'm leg-shackled to a philanderer? That hardly seems fair."

"You could have an affair with Lord Hayworth to spite me. I'm jesting!" he protested, even as she smacked him in the thigh with her gardening gloves.

"That's not funny!"

"Ow!" he said, laughing.

"It didn't hurt." She tried to scowl at him. "How's your arm?"

"Much better, thanks. Actually, that's why I came to see you. Somehow I forgot to tell you the most important thing about the duel. That I took your advice and apologized."

"I had heard that," she admitted with a begrudging smile. "'Twas very sensible of you."

"Well, I think it saved my life, so I owe you."

"You could buy me an ice cream sometime."

He smiled at her.

She smiled back, studying him. "What made you change your mind about apologizing to him?"

He pondered this. "Guilt. Pity. Remorse. A craven desire not to die."

"Well, I'm proud of you," she declared, though he wasn't sure for what. Then she paused. "I heard you met my friend Felicity—Miss Carvel. I heartily approve," she added. "She is the best of women."

He thought he detected the barest hint of jealousy in her voice, despite her praise for her friend.

Gable shrugged. "Even if she is, I'm not going anywhere near the girl. I have no desire to end up in another duel," he said with a shudder.

"How's that?" she asked in surprise.

"Friend of mine seems to have a prior claim of some sort."

"Really?" she exclaimed, and when he nodded in amusement, she narrowed her eyes. "Hmm. This friend wouldn't happen to be the Duke of Netherford, would it?"

"Aha, do you know something about it?" he asked in conspiratorial humor.

"Not a thing. But I've noticed they do react strangely to each other."

"I know!" He sat up straighter from his lazy pose. "You should've seen the look he gave me when I danced with her. You'd better not say anything to Miss Carvel about it, though."

"I don't dare. She's a little intimidating. Very prim and proper."

"She is a bit starchy, isn't she?" he agreed. "Of course, Netherford could make short work of that."

She giggled as she met his knowing glance.

"So here we are," Gable said quietly after a moment of sitting in companionable silence. He looked over at her. "I've missed you."

She looked sharply at him, as though startled by the admission, then she hesitated, nodding. "I've missed you, too."

They gazed at each other for a long moment.

"So where does that leave us?" she whispered.

"That is entirely up to you," he answered just as softly. "I still want to marry you." *More than ever.* "But please decide soon. I have less two and a half weeks left."

"Surely your father isn't really going to hold you to this arbitrary time limit."

"You don't know my father," he said. "The bills he brings up in Parliament are just a shadow of the innumerable laws that filled my childhood. Making the rules is what the Earl of Sefton does, dear. Believe me, it burns me to have to dance to his tune yet again. But then, I don't fancy penury." He glanced earnestly at her. "Please reconsider."

He could see she was weakening as she held his gaze for a heartbeat longer.

But then she sighed, looked away, and shook her head. "My lord, we've already discussed this. Frankly, it doesn't sound to me like you've even given these girls a chance. Not that I think it's wise to marry anyone for money, mind you, or even for a castle—yes, I know everybody does it, unless they get *really* lucky, like my sister. But if you want my advice, since it saved you last time, there you have it: Get to know these young ladies a bit better before you cast them all aside. Dig a little deeper."

"You don't understand, Katrina. If I start courting any one of them in earnest, next thing you know, there will be expectations. I don't want to do to some poor girl what Cecil Cooper did to you."

"Oh," she muttered. "Good point."

He rested his arm on the back of the bench and studied her, sensing progress. "You can see I'm out of my depth here. If you don't want me for yourself, won't you at least help me look? It could be fun," he said. "And your advice has already saved my life once, as you noted."

She looked at him incredulously. "You want me to help you pick a wife?"

"Why not? You could help me research...? Well, it's not as if you care who I marry!"

She scoffed and looked away. "That's not true and you know it."

"It seems true."

She turned to him again, looking vexed. "You think this is easy for me?"

"Isn't it?"

"No! You're very hard to say no to, actually," she said.

"Then say yes," he suggested in a murmur.

She gave him a subtle warning look and turned away, though the very air was charged between them.

He kept thinking of his dream, running his hands all over her body, making her gasp and heave with pleasure.

"You can change your mind, you know," he coaxed her. "That's what women *do*."

"I am not most women," she said in a tone as prickly as the nearby rosebushes, rich with leaves but not yet ready to bloom. "If you haven't noticed."

"Oh, I have. But I still don't understand."

"Yes, you do. You are merely being obtuse."

Now he was getting vexed, too. He sat up straight again. "I see. So the single life makes you so very happy?"

"It makes you happy, doesn't it?" she retorted.

The question took him off guard. Because the answer that sprang immediately to mind was not the one he would've expected only last week or the week before.

It dawned on him as they stared at each other, mutually irked, that all this time, all his conquests and peccadilloes had merely been a way to drown out the loneliness.

The bone-chilling realization quite routed him as the unsettling reality sank in. He looked away, shook his head, and rose. "Well, dear one, I don't wish to overstay my welcome." He turned around and sketched a bow. "Enjoy your day."

"Gable."

He turned with an inquiring look, his mask of mild-mannered savoir faire back firmly in place.

"Are you angry at me now?" she asked softly.

He succumbed to a rueful half-smile. "Never. But I do seem to get more than I bargained for whenever I see you, my fair neighbor."

"Here. Take this for your pains." She reached into the roomy pocket of her white work apron and handed him a delicate little sprig of forget-me-nots that she had clipped. "I was going to make a wee bouquet for my room, but you take it for your boutonniere. The blue will match your eyes. Get it into water soon," she added.

He took it from her with a wistful half-smile and tucked it into his buttonhole, a glimmer of roguery in his eyes. "I'd really rather have another kiss."

A startled laugh burst from her rosy lips. "Not from me!" she shot back as her cheeks turned pink.

"Your loss," he murmured with a smile, holding her gaze a moment longer in intimate remembrance of their kiss that enchanting night at the gazebo.

She seemed to be remembering it, too. He thrilled to the attraction that thrummed between them as she licked her lips unconsciously. The wave of desire passing behind her eyes hinted that at least she was tempted on that point. Well, of course, Gable thought wryly. That part had always been his forte.

He wondered, in a moment's fleeting cynical vanity, if perhaps she had taken his suggestion and asked one of his worldly ex-lovers what he was like in bed.

But on second thought, no. The virginal Katrina would be too embarrassed to ask anybody any such thing.

That's not why she wouldn't ask them, you idiot, his better sense muttered in the back of his mind, sounding rather exasperated with him. *She wouldn't ask because she wouldn't want to* know *about your escapades with other women.*

Because she cares for you. This one genuinely cares.

He could see it in her eyes, could feel it in his heart. And it shook him to the core. Did she even realize, come to think of it, that forget-me-nots symbolized steadfast love in the language of flowers?

Probably not.

With an awkward nod goodbye, he walked away, leaving Katrina to her garden.

But he pondered that wild, unsettling realization for the rest of the day. For he knew then that this one could love him...and it was very possible that he could love her, too.

Indeed, he feared a portion of him already did, and the implications of that tilted the whole damned planet off its axis for him.

That night, Gable stayed up late, took out his telescope, and tried to read his fate among the stars, to no avail. In the end, there was nothing to force his hand. Not destiny, not even his father. The choice was his alone—whether to give up his hedonistic ways and risk his heart or remain safely cynical, never knowing love.

Alone in the velvet darkness of the sparkling night, he still had no answers, but when a meteor streaked by, he bloody well wished on it.

Because you just never knew.

CHAPTER 5

Wedding Madness

he great day had arrived—and had nearly passed, by this hour—but Trinny still couldn't believe it. Her little sister had become a married woman.

Before her.

The reality of her decision not to marry, ever, was beginning to sink in after the beautiful ceremony at St. Andrew's on one end of Moonlight Square, and the packed reception at the Grand Albion on the other.

The Assembly Rooms were hot and the wine flowed freely, and everyone was there.

Abigail and Freddie were glowing, mingling among their countless guests. Mama was misty-eyed and slightly tipsy, hanging on to their precious bride and telling embarrassing childhood stories about her to anyone who'd listen.

As for Trinny, with her duties as maid of honor all but completed, she felt liberated after weeks of nonstop scrambling about on wedding business. Weeks of being at her mother's and sister's beck and call, ever since she had declared her spinsterhood and freed the happy couple to set the date.

It had been draining, exhausting. It had also been a gigantic distraction from her own life. Now that the orchestra was playing and the whole ordeal was close to being over, she was beginning to experience the first uneasy glimmerings of what existence would be like for her beyond this night. The long, lonely years ahead…

Another glass of wine helped her ignore the thought. Alas, it also made her slightly cheeky.

She was standing around chatting with a group of people, two of whom included Lord Sefton and his tall, handsome heir.

Gable was looking even more gorgeous than usual in his smart black-and-white evening attire, his ebony hair slicked back, not a one out of place. His nearness made her happy, though she hadn't had much chance to talk to him yet.

He had smiled at her in the church when she had walked down the aisle—alone—ahead of her sister and taken up her position off to the side, opposite Freddie's younger brother, the groomsman.

He seemed to like the way she looked in the pale pink dress her sister had chosen for her so that she'd match the blush-colored roses. It was very low-cut, but Abigail had always had a more daring sense of fashion than she did. Perhaps that helped explain why *she* hadn't had any trouble getting a man to fall in love with her…

Trinny suppressed a sigh, gulped a mouthful of wine, and met Gable's gaze as he stood on the other side of the group of people there chatting. He raised an eyebrow at her, swigging wine like a sailor, but suddenly, his father's polite monotone drew her attention.

"Congratulations, Lady Beresford," Lord Sefton said to Mama. "Your daughter and new son-in-law look very happy together."

"That's because they're very much in love," Trinny piped up, slurring slightly, with an edge of reproach in her tone for the old bully. "People should marry for love, not money, don't you think, m'lord?"

Gable choked on his wine.

His father frowned at her, taken aback by her impertinence.

She waited expectantly for the mighty earl's answer, but everyone else around them shuffled and looked at their feet, since money matches were the done thing across all Society.

Well, it seemed she'd killed another conversation. But what else did they expect from the odd duck of the family?

"Er, Katrina, dear!" Mama said, flashing an apologetic smile around at her guests. "Go tell the staff we need more roast beef brought out. The buffet table seems to be running low."

She looked at her mother indignantly. The countess sent her a glare that said, *Rudesby!*

"Yes, Mama," she muttered. But she sent Lord Sefton a warning look before she obeyed, letting her friend's overbearing father know that she, for one, was aware of his bullying and did not at all approve of the ultimatum he had given his son.

"Humph." Pivoting on her heel, she marched off, though she winced with every step. She'd been on her feet for many hours and the slight heels on the pink-dyed shoes her sister had chosen for her were pinching her toes.

She looked around for a servant to whom she could pass along her mother's request—*if* more roast beef was even needed. *She probably just wanted to get rid of me*, Trinny thought, on the verge of moping but only because the wine had made her a little emotional.

In any case, all the waiters and footmen she saw were already busy helping other guests. *Very well, I'll tell them myself. A spinster daughter is little more than a servant, anyway.*

You brought it on yourself.

Oh, leave me alone! she told her brain. *The wine was supposed to shut you up, anyway.*

With a sigh, she headed for the service door off the ballroom. Behind it lay a little walk-through anteroom, where the hotel's efficient staff put everything they might quickly need to grab: waiting rolls of silverware in napkins, stacks of extra plates of various sizes, a tower of clean wineglasses, rags for cleaning up the tables, pitchers of water, and...

Aha!

A big barrel of ice with a treasure trove of open wine bottles left to breathe for a bit before being served.

Her glass now empty, Trinny helped herself to a bottle; hefting it by the neck, she marched on toward the door at the other end of the service passage. It opened onto a dim wooden stairwell. She could hear a clamor from below that told her this was, indeed, the way to the kitchens.

Feet smarting, she walked down the creaky steps until she reached the huge, crazed kitchens. She beckoned to a plump, harried-looking woman who seemed to be in charge.

"So sorry to bother you. More roast beef upstairs, I'm told."

"Ach, you shouldn't have had to trouble yerself, miss! Couldn't you find one of the waiters to tell?" the cook cried, looking aghast to assume the staff was not attending properly to the guests.

"No, no! They were all busy taking care of others. The truth is, I suppose I just wanted a few minutes of peace and quiet. I'm the maid of honor, you see. And I'm exhausted. Would you mind terribly if I took a wee break down here somewhere out of the way?"

"Make yourself at home, dearie," the woman said, clearly relieved. "There's a stool in the pantry where you can put your feet up if ye like."

"Bless you!" Trinny said, following her gesture toward the open doorway across from the bottom of the stairs.

As she shuffled toward the pantry to get out of everybody's way, she felt the cool night breeze wafting in from the service door to the terrace straight ahead, between the pantry and the bottom of the stairs.

She glanced out at the gardens beyond the terrace, but nobody was out there. The stone benches looked appealing, but the thought of sitting alone in the dark was a little more solitude than she desired.

She was already feeling a bit depressed, cut off from the world by this single state she had embraced. She did not wish to put herself even farther from the ordinary course of life. She preferred to stay here, close to the comforting bustle of human activity at the edge of the kitchens.

Honestly, though, it was a relief to escape the worried scrutiny of all her relatives and neighbors upstairs for a while, all of whom she just *knew* secretly pitied her.

Upon entering the pantry, she plopped down onto the stool she found there, and the first thing she did was take off her shoes and flex her aching feet. "Ahh."

The kitchen's flagstone floor was cool and soothing to the sole, she thought with a tipsy chuckle. Then she refilled her empty wineglass from the bottle she'd purloined.

After swallowing another gulp, she let out a weary sigh and leaned back against the cabinets. The clamor of the kitchen was muffled in her little hideaway, and she savored this moment to catch her breath in utter luxury. She probably should've invited Abigail to join her, for her poor sister had been onstage all day, as it were.

I'm glad I'll never be a bride, Trinny thought. *Too much work!*

She closed her eyes, waiting for the feeling to return to her toes. Aside from her throbbing feet, the rest of her was tingling from the wine. She'd surely suffer the headache tomorrow, but for now, the pleasant buzz in her head blurred her messy emotions, which made no sense to her right now, anyway.

Her heart was all mixed up today, both happy and sad, poignant and wistful. And behind it all, a slight panic had begun to percolate in the back of her mind, screeching at her, *What have I done to my life?*

Was this *really* what she wanted? Never to be the lady of the house? Never to be a mother? A grandmother someday?

Because if not, she could still change her mind. She had a gorgeous, charming man—with a castle—interested in marrying her. Making her his countess.

You don't have to be alone, you quiz.

But don't you see? I will be, if I marry him. Even more alone than if I were single, because we would live under the same roof but…he would never love me. Not the way that I'd love him, with everything I've got.

No, I couldn't bear it.

"So, there you are," a droll voice said. "What is going on in here, dare I ask?"

She opened her eyes and found Gable leaning in the doorway, looking debonair, and studying her in amusement.

"Are we hiding?" he inquired.

"No," she said, though not too convincingly. "We're just taking a break. And drinking." She reached for the bottle and topped off her glass again. "Lots of drinking."

"Well, you shouldn't drink alone. Can I join the party?"

"Of course you may, dear fellow. But only if you don't try to make me put my shoes back on." She straightened both legs until her bare feet peeked out from underneath the hem of her gown. "See?"

He flashed a roguish grin as he joined her in the narrow pantry. "Put those darling things away before I bite them."

"Ew! You're mad."

"I mean it."

"I suppose you probably do, knowing you." Laughing, she offered him the bottle. He grasped it by the neck and took a swig, then loosened his cravat. "Mmm, that's good. What is it, a Riesling?"

She shrugged. "I don't know, but I warn ye, it goes down easy," she declared, slurring ever so slightly.

He leaned against the cabinets in an idle pose and studied her in amusement. He smelled good, she thought as she inhaled the enticing scent of his cologne in the close confines of the pantry, then she let out a sigh and rubbed the back of her neck.

"So what did you want, anyway? Did they need me for something again?" She paused and frowned. "Did my mother send you to find me?"

"What, you think I'm a spy for the enemy? Now I'm offended."

She grinned at his jest. "Actually, I came to give you a round of applause for what you said to my father." A look of rich satisfaction crept across his chiseled face as he set the bottle on the cabinet and began clapping slowly for her. "God, that was utterly delicious."

She let out a gleeful laugh and swung her feet. "Wasn't it, though?

You're very welcome, my friend! Somebody had to stand up to him."

"Hear, hear. He didn't know what hit him."

"Unfortunately, I don't think I made a very good impression." She giggled again, and Gable grinned.

"Ah, don't worry. He finds fault with everyone."

"I really don't know what came over me. Must've been the wine talking."

"Well, I thought it was your finest moment—and you have a lot of those." He toasted her with the bottle, and they both took another swallow, then lapsed into a brief, companionable silence.

"So how are you?" he murmured, eyeing her shrewdly.

"Worn *out*," she said. "I had no idea that getting a sister married off would be such a grueling ordeal. Do you realize I'll still have to go through this four more times over the years? For Martha, Gwendolyn, Betsy, and Jane. All this effort for a mere few hours! Honestly, if it were me, I'd rather elope."

"Me too," he agreed.

"Not that it matters," she reminded him with a pointed look.

He heaved a long-suffering sigh. "Well, congratulations anyway, love. You survived it."

"Thank you," she replied, and took another swallow of wine.

"Are you *sure* you're all right?" he persisted in a diplomatic tone a few seconds later. "I saw you crying earlier today. I was worried. I hate it when you cry."

She looked at him in surprise. "Everybody cries at weddings. Don't they?"

He merely arched a brow, studying her.

"I'm fine! Those were tears of happiness, I swear."

"Is that why you're in here getting drunk?" he asked softly.

"Oh, leave me alone," she mumbled with a scowl. "I never said I was perfect."

"Imperfection is one of your dearest qualities. Talk to me," he cajoled her.

"What is there to say?" she burst out. "I'm already...overloaded! My heart hurts from feeling too much today. My head's a tangle. I don't want to feel anymore tonight. I don't want to think."

Gable paused for a long moment, then moved closer. "Well, I can help you with that."

"Hey!" she protested as he lifted her wineglass out of her hand, setting it aside. "I was enjoying that!"

"You'll enjoy this, too. Trust me," he said in a husky voice, leaning down before her chair. With a gentle pressure of his fingertips under her chin, he raised her head and kissed her—a soft, satin caress of his mouth on hers.

A sigh escaped her, and her aching toes curled where she sat.

As his lips lingered on hers, she held perfectly still, breathless.

Then he pulled back a small space. "Let me take care of you, Katrina."

At his whisper, she somehow found the strength to open her eyes after the silken spell he'd cast on her. Holding his gaze, she was not sure what he meant by that, but she was desperately eager all of a sudden to find out.

"My lord." She looked away in trembling confusion, cheeks flaming with heat. The pantry was spinning. "They say wine makes girls lose their inhibitions, then they become prey to wicked rakehells. Are you trying to take advantage of me?"

"Would you like me to?" he whispered.

She swallowed hard and stared at him as her will drained away. "God, *yes*." Then, in the privacy of that little pantry, she moved into his arms, past caring. She didn't stop to question what she was doing. She just wanted another taste of his beautiful mouth.

He lifted her up in his arms and set her on the countertop formed by the lower row of cabinets. She slid her arms around his neck and returned his fevered kisses with abandon.

Mmm, you taste so good, she wanted to tell him, but she couldn't speak with his tongue swirling its magical dance in her mouth.

Though the swift but hungry exchange soon left them both panting, neither of them had any desire to make a spectacle of themselves in front of the staff of the Grand Albion.

Gable lifted her hand to his lips. "Come with me," he ordered in a gravelly tone.

"Where?" she whispered, heart pounding as he helped her down from the countertop. He did not let go of her hand.

"You'll see. Come on. You don't even have to wear your shoes," he added, sending her a seductive smile over his shoulder as he headed for the doorway.

"Gable, where are you going?" she whispered insistently as she followed him, holding on to his hand, both worried and enchanted.

"I'm spiriting you away, my darling. Come." Then he stepped through the door that opened onto the terrace.

She followed him outside into the dark with a thrill in her blood like nothing she had ever known before.

They didn't go far.

Outside, the flagstones were even cooler underfoot than in the kitchen, and the starlight glimmered over the fragrant gardens. But Gable led her discreetly around the nearby corner of the building, where the terrace wrapped around the side of the hotel for just a few feet.

Completely out of sight, he drove her back against the wall, and then he kissed her in earnest.

Reckless passion poured from him as he leaned against her, grasped her hips, and moved his hard, lean body against her in the most tempting fashion while his kiss consumed her. It was shocking—and absolutely wonderful. A heady groan escaped her with the overwhelming realization of just how sincerely Gable wanted her.

And he was true to his word. His ardent efforts really did erase every last sane, rational thought and irksome worry from her mind, transporting her senses far, far away to some lovely, wicked dreamland.

She clung to him, lost in sensation and raw desire as he teased her lips with his kisses and held her pinned against the wall. It was exactly where she wanted to be.

"Feeling better yet?" he breathed between kisses.

"Much," she gasped out.

He gave her an impossibly seductive half-smile, his face shadowed, roguery sparkling in his eyes. Then he came at her again. She let him do to her as he pleased, heart slamming with delight as he captured her lower lip between his teeth and licked at it, made love to it, ravished every inch of it. His hands glided down the curves of her neck, bringing her skin to life. His fingers trailed along her collarbones as he kissed her throat, and then his touch moved lower to explore her chest.

"I've been watching you all night, wanting to devour you," he panted at her earlobe. "You're so beautiful. You move me so, Katrina. I want you to the marrow of my bones."

"Oh, Gable." The next thing she knew, he had freed her breast from the low-cut décolletage of her gown, and her soft flesh was in his hand. He lowered himself to his knees and took the fiery, stiffened peak into his mouth, feeding on her. He grasped her hips and caressed her.

Trinny was enraptured. She couldn't believe this was happening, but she had no desire to stop. Resting her hands on his broad shoulders to steady herself, she couldn't help but appreciate the size and strength of him compared to her, the stalwart dominance of his muscled frame.

It would be an easy thing for him to overpower her and take her here against the wall, whether she wanted it or not, but she knew in her core that this man would never do such a thing. In a haze of sensuality, she cupped his sculpted face and watched him sucking on her nipple. In that moment, she wanted to give him everything she was. She felt so close to him, as though she had been made for him, here in the shadows of their secret world, silvered with moonlight.

Meanwhile, Gable's warm, smooth hand had slipped beneath her skirts. Trinny swallowed hard as she felt his fingers gliding up her calf, playing at her knee. She widened her stance slightly as she leaned against the wall, parting her legs for him instinctively, her fingers digging into his shoulders in building excitement. When his palm skimmed slowly up her thigh with a touch so warm and sure, she closed her eyes in agonized anticipation.

Chest heaving, she rested her head against the stone wall, biting back a moan of pleasure as his silken touch slid along the juncture of her thighs. He groaned to find her already slippery wet with need. Then he began to stroke her there as he nestled his face against her breasts. She arched her back and moved with his touch, unable to stop herself. Her flesh craved something her mind did not yet understand. All she could do was clasp his strong shoulders and let him pleasure her while her pulse thundered like a summer storm.

"Come for me, Katrina," he whispered raggedly after several moments. "You need this, I know. It's all right. You don't have to be shy with me."

He kissed the valley between her breasts and pressed his fingers into her more deeply, but this combined with the way the heel of his hand also chafed beguilingly against her mound was more than she could withstand.

She held on to his head and ran her fingers through his hair as the masterful seducer coaxed her to the brink of surrender. A cry of passion tore from her lips. Flaming release pulsed through her and ran down every nerve ending, shattering her, body and soul, into the light of a million stars. The frantic tremors eased after a long moment, and she was left panting and dazed, her emotions surprisingly raw, even more so than before.

Gable silently rose to his feet and gathered her into his arms. He kissed her forehead but didn't say a word. Apparently, even the rakehell's glib charm had failed him in the sudden intensity of their encounter.

She rested her head against his chest and could feel his heart throbbing through his elegant attire. Finally, she looked up and met his gaze, a little self-conscious despite his tender assurance that she needn't feel shy with him.

Neither of them spoke. His eyes, so soulful, said it all. They told her that although he was still powerfully aroused, he, too, sensed that there was something going on here between them much deeper than desire.

She reached up and cupped his face, drawing him down to kiss her.

His lips met hers gently, but he ended the kiss in the next moment, as though he couldn't stop gazing into her eyes. "You're really beautiful," he whispered, sounding almost wistful.

"I am?" she breathed, trying to believe.

"Oh yes." He tucked a stray lock of her hair behind her ear as he stared at her, his eyes glimmering in the night with a sort of newfound wonder, and, in that moment, it seemed like nothing could ever break this spell between them...

Except something did.

A force from outside their blissful little world.

"Roland!" a man's voice called from the vicinity of the terrace in a loud stage whisper. "Are you out here? Damn it, man, where are you?"

Gable glanced over, furrowing his brow. "That sounds like Sidney. Hold that thought," he whispered, then went to the edge of the building and peered around the corner.

"Sid? What is it?" Apparently confirming it was friend, he stepped into view. "I'm here. What's afoot?"

"There you are! God, I've been looking everywhere for you!"

"Why?"

"I'm trying to save your neck, that's why." Footfalls clicked closer, still out of sight. Though Lord Sidney had spoken in a low tone, Trinny could still hear him.

She hastened to pull her bodice back up and smoothed her skirts, checking to make sure all her bits were covered. With Gable gone, she let out a long, steadying exhalation, giddy after their antics. Nevertheless, she took care to eavesdrop.

"What's going on?" Gable queried, still in view by the corner of the building.

"Just in case you're out here with a woman, I thought I'd better warn you there's another one looking for you—no, two. No, actually, make that three."

This got Trinny's full attention. She tore her dreamy gaze off the constellations twinkling in the dark sky overhead and glanced toward the conversation, furrowing her brow.

Gable's spine had stiffened; he must've known she was hearing this, though Lord Sidney spoke in a low tone.

"The Countess of Pelletier expects you to dance with her daughter for some reason, and that red-haired baroness you were fooling with last month apparently wants to strangle you—I've no idea why. All three of them are searching the premises for you, and they're starting to get suspicious. So I suggest you and your *femme du jour* either hie yourselves out of here while you still can, or part ways before you get caught and hurry back to the ballroom before you cause a scandal. I don't want m' mate getting shot again," he added.

"Thanks," Gable said grimly.

"Do you want me to wait for you? We can walk around the building and go in the front together, say we were both outside having a smoke. You've vouched for me enough times, God knows."

"All right, yes, thanks. I'll need a moment. Head them off if they come this way."

"Done," Sidney said.

Trinny stood there, wide-eyed with shock.

Oh, the life of a rakehell, she thought as disillusionment cascaded through her body with a chill that chased away the lingering traces of pleasure.

You fool, she said to herself as Gable returned to their little hiding place.

"It seems my absence has been noted. Yours will be, too, soon, if it hasn't been already. Sid's right. We should really get back inside."

"Of course," Trinny mumbled, confounded.

He adjusted himself, smoothed his hair, tugged his clothes into place, and then gestured for her to go ahead of him.

Ever the gentleman.

You pig, she thought, but bit her tongue, fearful that she'd say something she'd regret on account of the wine that had already proved to make her cheeky.

Numb, she walked on, still barefoot. But with every step, her indignation grew.

Viscount Sidney, tall and blond and handsome, arched a brow at her in amusement as she passed.

"I'll be right with you," Gable murmured to his fellow rakehell.

"Take your time." Sidney lit a cheroot and sauntered off politely across the terrace. Perhaps he had seen the glimmer of wrath in Trinny's eyes when she had glanced at him and realized if he valued his safety, he should probably move away.

God, they had their systems, didn't they? She shook her head, astonished at how these rogues all covered for one another, smooth as clockwork.

Masters of the Earth. If they treated women this way as bachelors, no wonder Parliament was such a mess when they got to the House of Lords.

The tight leash she was trying to keep on her temper pulled away from her. She pivoted outside the screened door. "Can I just ask you one question?"

In the dim glow of the light coming from the kitchens, Gable seemed to brace himself. "Yes?"

"How many women have you brought to that spot before me? Or have you lost count? I mean, you knew exactly where to go."

He blanched. "It isn't like that."

"Really? And why would the Countess of Pelletier be expecting you to dance with her daughter, Gable, hmm? The other one he mentioned doesn't surprise me, of course—the married one, I mean. That's your favorite prey!"

"Katrina—"

"What an exciting life you lead, my lord!" she flung at him in mocking humor. "How very picaresque!" She shook her head at him, turning away. "You disgust me."

She heard him snort as she started to walk away.

"Well, you didn't look too disgusted a few minutes ago," he drawled.

She whirled around, astounded. "Oh, throw it in my face, why don't you?" She could feel a burning blush flooding into her cheeks as she huffed with affront. "That was only because of the wine!"

"No, it wasn't," Gable said serenely.

"Yes, it was! You...you took advantage of me in my intoxicated state!"

"Ha. You wanted me," he whispered.

"So?" Her blush deepened. She probably looked like a strawberry right now, but it seemed a little late for modesty. "Everybody wants you! What news is there in that? At least *now* I'm sober! Funny how a few choice revelations can snap a person right back to reality!"

"Please calm down—"

"*Don't* tell me to calm down!" she thundered at him as loudly as she dared, only belatedly dropping her voice to a furious whisper. "You are *unbelievable*. Do you think I don't know what you're up to?"

"Uh, what am I up to?" he echoed, furrowing his brow.

She narrowed her eyes at him. "Don't try to look innocent! There is nothing innocent about you."

"Katrina, just because those women are looking for me doesn't mean I care to see *them*."

"Just stop, please!" she begged him in anguish. "I see exactly what you're doing!"

"Then enlighten me!" he barked. "Because I have no blasted idea what you are talking about. *I* thought I was simply out here enjoying the company of the girl I want to marry."

She flinched. "You see? There it is. Your lying, treacherous little plan!"

Gable shook his head, looking bewildered.

"Do I have to spell it out for you? That's all this was about, and I fell for it! You don't care about *me*. All you care about is the money a-and the castle you stand to lose! Oh, you'd *prefer* me as your countess because we usually tolerate each other's company well enough—"

"I think we do more than tolerate—"

"But just in case you can't charm me into doing your will," she said, ignoring his attempt to speak, "you've got Lady Pelletier's little henwit of a daughter lined up as your second choice. You're as bad as Cecil Cooper, doing the same thing to that poor young girl as he did to me. Leading her on in case nothing better comes along. I'm not stupid!"

"Now, hold on right there," he said, his usually unflappable expression forming into one of wrath. "I have never falsely led a woman on in my entire life! You had better watch what you're accusing me of, my lady. There is a limit to the insults I will tolerate, even from you."

"You two sound like you're already married," Sidney remarked.

"Shut up!" they both ordered him in unison.

Then Trinny fixed Gable with a withering stare. "Go, run along, and find your little bride, then. I'm sure your father will be pleased. The Pelletier girl can have you for all I care! You're not worth the lifetime of heartache you'd inevitably bring me."

"Why do you assume that?" he exclaimed. "What have I ever done to hurt you in the time you've known me?"

"Well, nothing yet—but a leopard doesn't change his spots!"

"I am not a leopard," he said through gritted teeth.

"You're a rake. So how could I ever trust you? I mean, look at what you just did with me tonight! You brought me out here to try to seduce me into going along with your plan, didn't you? Thought you'd give me a taste of the pleasure you're so good at, just to maneuver me into place so you can get your own way."

"That's not true."

But she didn't believe him. She was too angry at him for being unwilling to offer her a proper marriage that she suddenly could hardly bear the sight of the man.

"At least now I know the sorts of things you do with those other ladies. And, as you've said, you have no intention of stopping. So, you see? If I agreed to your plan, I would never know when you were lying, when you were telling the truth, what game you were playing, or most importantly, who you were with on any given occasion."

"Katrina—"

"I can never agree to that. Why on earth would I do that to myself?" She shook her head, staring at him. "Why does *any* woman ever marry a rakehell? I'd rather be alone."

He flinched at her words. "Then you will be, and I hope it's everything you dreamed of!" he yelled.

"Damn," Sidney muttered in the background as Trinny sent Gable one last furious glare and blasted through the door.

Heart pounding, stomach in knots, she ducked into the pantry to grab her shoes, then peered out again only to say, "Whatever this was between us, it's *over*. Don't call on me again."

"Don't worry, I won't!"

Then she slammed the kitchen door in his face and pounded up the stairwell, shaking from head to toe.

# # #

Gable stood there, stunned. *What the hell just happened?*

His friend let out a low whistle. "Little fireball, that one." Sid sauntered over, studying him with a curious look askance. "Wasn't that Beresford's eldest daughter?"

Gable nodded, in a daze.

"Hmm," Sidney said.

"What?" Gable ground out.

Sid shrugged in his nonchalant way. "Not that it's any of my business, but, er...*why* in the *hell* are you out here fooling around with a virgin? Have you lost your mind?"

"Apparently so," Gable muttered. *Because I want her like I've never wanted anyone before.*

"Careful, mate," Sid warned. "I fear wedding madness has got to you."

Gable glanced at him regretfully, then shook his head in distraction. "I don't think that's it."

Wedding madness on its own couldn't cause the bizarre heartache that filled him after Katrina's shocking decree, banishing him from her life.

No, he feared the sickness was something far worse.

Bloody goddamn love.

To a rakehell, the disease usually proved fatal.

CHAPTER 6

A Farewell

*T*he room spun when Trinny awoke the next morning. The cheery tweeting of the birds outside felt like pins being driven into her ears. Her head thumped mercilessly, and her mouth was as dry as if she'd been eating shredded paper all night long.

Oh God. She tried to sit up but failed, and she pressed a hand to her brow as she lay back down, feeling positively awful.

It took her a moment to get her bearings. *Lud, I'd never make it as a rakehell.*

And that thought suddenly recalled what had transpired last night between her and Gable. Her stomach immediately lurched, and she squeezed her eyes shut as it all came flooding back.

In an instant, the memories chased away the blissful forgetfulness of her dead drunken sleep.

Oh no…

She remembered the way he had touched her and kissed her, pressed her against the wall of the Grand Albion.

And then she remembered their fight.

She flicked her eyes open and stared dizzily at the rotating ceiling. Horrified regret paralyzed her. *How could I say those things? How could I tell him never to call on me again?*

Forget that, her better sense opined. *How could you let him put his hands up your dress? His mouth on your cleavage?*

Oh God. Her pulse was now pounding with panic. What if that brash moment of moon madness had been found out? Was she ruined even now?

Could a spinster even *be* ruined?

The queasiness intensified. Because, right now, the only thing worse than indeed never seeing him again would be finding out their tryst had been discovered and then being *forced* to marry him—given the awful way they had left things between them.

Oh no, no, nooo. The thought kept repeating in her mind, along with, *I'm never drinking again!*

But after a momentary panic, Trinny realized her mother would not have left her sleeping the night away if Society had found out about how she and Lord Roland had slipped away together during the wedding.

She must be in the clear, for she'd have been instantly awakened and forced to face her parents' wrath. So she was probably safe, thank God.

Still, it was hard to feel any genuine relief when she recalled her ugly fight with Gable. Had she really banished her handsome friend from her life?

She sat up in bed, feeling as though she might throw up at the memory.

Was it too late to plead innocent, blame it on the wine? *In vino veritas?* But her heart sank, because the old maxim held water. Every harsh word she'd said to Gable had been true.

That was the most sickening part of all. Knowing she had made the right decision by pushing him away. She had to stand her ground and let him go. It would hurt less that way.

She was surprised at the tears that flooded into her eyes, considering how desiccated she was from the wine. She closed her eyes and lay back down, trembling. Then she pulled her pillow over her face to muffle a sob of despair.

# # #

Across the square, Gable had also awakened, but he was not suffering any aftereffects, as he hadn't overindulged. But he felt nearly as ill as he supposed—and hoped—Trinny did, for different reasons.

Gable was still angry. The first thought in *his* mind when his eyes flicked open was, *How dare she accuse me of such dishonorable dealings?*

Who did the little quiz think she was?

He had been hurt, bewildered, indignant, and then mad as hell when she had kicked him out of her life last night. Being ordered to go to the devil, being rejected and sent away, was not exactly something he was used to from the fair sex.

Frankly, he was used to them doting on him. Treating him like he could do no wrong. But this one... Gable shook his head as he sat up.

So she refused to see the benefits to the offer he had proposed, though they were manifold. To hell with her, then. He hoped she regretted her foolishness this morning to the bottom of her vain heart.

Indeed, he hoped she came round groveling, because he couldn't wait to tell her it was too late. That he had pledged himself to another. Which he meant to do first thing today.

Hell, he'd toss the bloody names into a hat and pick one out at random, just to spite her. Then she'd be sorry.

Except he doubted she would care.

As he rose from his bed and went about his morning ablutions with a glower, he could not help feeling a little used, frankly. The little hussy had allowed him to pleasure her, then sent him away.

He growled under his breath, raking his comb roughly through his hair. He nearly bit his valet's head off when the man came to help him dress.

"Go away!"

"Yes, sir! Apologies, my lord."

He dressed himself in a rage, making a muck of three cravats in a row before giving up on a neckcloth entirely, crumpling up the one he held, and throwing it aside in disgust.

It was easier to be furious than to let himself feel what lay beyond the anger.

As he sat down to put on his shoes, glaring at the floor in a brown study, he could not help wondering uncomfortably if this was how some of the women he'd dallied with had felt afterward. If so, then it seemed the proverbial boot was on the other leg.

The fitting old maxim so annoyed him that he hurled his shoe across the room, where it crashed against the wall and left a black streak, and as a consequence, he both scared the dickens out of his servants downstairs and burdened them with needless work.

But what did a selfish rakehell care?

Jaw clenched, Gable prowled downstairs, heading for the morning room and his breakfast. As he traversed the gleaming, quiet halls of his bachelor refuge, his fine terrace house seemed remarkably large this morning for some strange reason. Maybe he was merely hungry, but it seemed a longer walk today than usual from his chamber to the breakfast table.

He stopped in the marble-floored corridor, struck by the stillness. His house was so quiet…all the elegant rooms seemed ever so empty.

A little unnerved, he hurried on.

Before he even arrived at the morning room, though, he could already feel a disturbing change taking place in his emotions. The anger was giving way to sorrow.

Regret.

Dangerous guests to entertain and very unpleasant first thing in the morning.

He sat down at the table, then stared unseeingly at the newspaper his butler handed to him, already folded open to the sports page.

When his plate was set before him, he looked at it and wasn't sure he could eat it in the wave of sickening disgust that washed over him.

Self-disgust.

Because she's right, came the blunt thought. *That* is *who I am. That is what I do.*

And in fact he *had* brought women to that spot before.

You're exactly right about me, Trinny.

And suddenly it seemed to Gable that he had much bigger problems than having his funds cut off.

He set the newspaper aside and then slowly scanned the table. It was a round table, meant for a family. Or at least a husband and wife, but he sat here alone every day, and the fact was, he had relished it, had treasured his bachelor sanctuary here.

Until this very moment. And now, with no warning, it had just become unbearable.

He pushed away from the table and rose. "Think I'll eat at the club this morning," he told his bewildered staff.

Then he left in a hurry.

# # #

Gable took care to remain in the company of his rakehell friends around the clock for the next two days. Rogues, scoundrels, and hedonists all, they distracted him, made him laugh, got him drunk, didn't ask what the hell was wrong. Didn't even notice anything was wrong, probably. But then, Gable always had been a fairly smooth liar.

On the third night, at an expensive but disreputable establishment called the Satin Slipper, the lads were lounging around wasting time and watching the scantily clad girls dance and writhe.

Netherford had captured one of them on his lap, and she was feeding him strawberries from the refreshment table as though he were a sultan. Sidney, meanwhile, had made a game of things, as was his way, trying to catch the berries in his mouth as his favorite courtesan laughingly tossed them to him from across the room. He kept missing, as his reflexes were not exactly sharp after all their drinking.

Oh, it was great fun, Gable thought darkly.

If you were seventeen.

Unfortunately, he could feel a saturnine mood, cold and dark, settling over him. He glanced at Netherford in annoyance. The Duke of Scandal was in his own world, hair mussed, cravat undone, the courtesan teasing him with cherries now, passed from her lips to his.

"So, Netherford," Gable spoke up in an almost surly tone, "what's going on between you and Felicity Carvel?"

The sound of that name had a curious effect upon His Grace. It so startled him that he seemed to swallow a cherry pit, choking on it slightly. Recovering in a heartbeat, he dropped the harlot off his lap, sat bolt upright in his chair, and glanced around wildly. "What? Where?"

"Hey!" the girl yelled from the floor.

Gable arched a brow at his friend. "She's not *here*, man. We're in a brothel, remember?"

Netherford scowled at him. "You nearly killed me."

"Well? What's going on between you two?"

"Nothing!" he said, quite unconvincingly. He scoffed as Sidney dashed over to play the hero and dotingly picked up the dropped harlot off the floor.

"There, there, dear little darling," he soothed in merry gallantry, dusting off her shapely bottom for her. "What a rudesby! Come sit with me, poor thing. I may not be a duke, but I will be a marquess when my old man turns up his toes, and you know I'd never drop you..."

"Thank you, my lord. At least *someone* here's a gentl'man." She draped her arms around the waist of the golden-haired charmer, who winked at them over his shoulder as he stole her away.

Netherford made no effort to stop his plaything from escaping, for the mention of Miss Carvel seemed to have taken all the fun out of other female company for him.

He eyed Gable in suspicion. "Why do you ask me such a thing?" he demanded.

"No reason," he answered mildly, and the way his friend furrowed his brow and turned away in distraction disturbed him, for the look on Netherford's face seemed to express exactly the same sort of inward tug-of-war that Gable was feeling.

In any case, the duke didn't protest when another pretty creature sidled over to show him her wares. Ignoring Gable now, Naughty Netherford passed a lazy glance over her, offering her a hand as she lowered herself onto his lap.

"And what's your name, lovely?" he asked, as if it mattered.

And all of a sudden, Gable was done.

Absolutely finished. With all of it. He just wanted out of here. Out of this place. Out of this life.

He didn't even finish his drink. Heart pounding, he set it aside, stood, bade his friends farewell, slung his coat over his shoulder, and marched out, sickened by it all. He couldn't stand another minute of that mode of existence.

Outside, the fresh night air helped to clear his head.

Then it was a quiet drive home in his phaeton. It was lonely, but he didn't mind. The streets were deserted, the serene gibbous moon riding high.

When he got home, he retired, but before lying down, he stepped out onto the balcony off his bedchamber to gaze at the night, mentally marking the occasion.

His last night on earth as a rakehell.

Then he went back inside. *Good riddance.*

With that, he blew out the candle and went to bed. But as soon as his head hit the pillow, thoughts of *her* were not far from his mind. He folded his arms beneath his head and stared into the darkness.

You were right about me, Trinny. I see that now. But you were wrong about one thing…

A leopard can *change his spots.*

You'll see.

# # #

"To what do I owe this honor?" his father drawled when Gable called on him the next day. "If you've come to plead for more time, I am not in a giving mood."

"No, sir," he said. "I haven't come to plead for anything."

"Good," his father said, all business, as usual. He sat back down at his desk. "Then how goes the search?"

"That's what I came to speak to you about, sir."

"Well?"

Gable paced back and forth across his father's office once or twice before he found the nerve to state his decision out loud. "Father, I'm going to ask for the hand of Lord Beresford's eldest daughter, Lady Katrina. But...there is a good chance she'll say no," he added in a taut voice. "And if that is the case, I've come to say I accept your pronouncement to cut off my funds." He shrugged. "I really can't blame you. But I can't marry someone else for convenience's sake when I...I..." His words trailed off, and silence hung between them.

His father slowly arched a brow. "I see," he murmured, looking fascinated. "Well, well."

"I also want to apologize to you, sir, for any...disappointment that I've caused you over the years...with my, er, prior mode of life. But I want you to know, everything has changed."

"Indeed?" The earl stared at him in shock, as though he feared he might be sleeping and this was naught but a strange dream.

"Yes. I don't expect you to believe, but you'll see." Gable dropped his gaze, self-conscious. "That is all, sir. I know you are a very busy man, so I shall endeavor not to waste your time. Good day." He bowed to him and retreated.

"Isn't she the saucy one from the wedding?" his father said behind him, still sounding mystified.

Gable paused, facing the door.

"The young lady who thinks that all the world should wed for love?"

His back still to his father, a rueful smile spread across Gable's lips at the memory of how she had shocked some of the stuffing out of his stuffy Lord Sefton.

He turned back and nodded. "Aye, sir. She's the one," he said with quiet, meaningful force.

"I see." His father looked terribly amused; understanding glinted in his eyes. "Well! Good luck, son. I hope she takes your offer. Since there is a castle at stake, after all," he added with a subtle note of knowing humor in his voice.

"For the record, that has nothing to do with it," Gable said quietly.

"That is your own affair. Do let me know if we have happy news, hmm?"

Gable nodded wryly and crossed the office, wondering in hindsight if he'd misjudged his father all along. He was beginning to see that his father was just looking out for him, in his own, domineering way. But whatever the earl's limitations, he was merely a concerned parent and had meant it for good.

Indeed, perhaps all of his father's sober hard work had merely filled Gable with self-recrimination, and that was why he had chafed under his authority. But perhaps there was some small way he could make it up to the man.

He paused when he reached the office door and turned around. "By the way, Father, I seem to have a lot of free time on my hands these days. If there's anything I can do to help you with your work, I should like to be of use."

Lord Sefton once again looked astounded. He all but pinched himself. "Er, yes, actually. If you can get a few of your friends with seats in the Lords to attend the session next week, I could use their votes on my bill."

"I can do that," Gable said smoothly. "Do you have an extra copy of the latest draft? I'm better at persuading if I know what I'm talking about."

"I'll have one sent over to you this afternoon." His father seemed to marvel at this transformation. "Thank you, son."

"That's what family is for," Gable answered with a warm but guarded smile. Then he showed himself out.

He was quite tickled by how well that had gone. The amazement on his father's face was almost worth all the annoyance his old man had caused him over the years. But although he walked out feeling that his meeting with His Lordship had gone better than expected, now came the real test. He braced himself for his next appointment with destiny.

Facing his father had always been a little nerve-racking, but at least he usually knew what to expect. His next mission, by contrast, was fraught with perilous unknowns. He was indeed venturing into terra incognita, even though it would take place on the well-trodden ground of his club.

A short while later, Gable resolutely strode into the Grand Albion, dry-mouthed, his heart racing.

Since it was only ten o'clock in the morning, none of his set was there yet. They wouldn't wander in until late in the afternoon.

Instead, this was the respectable time of day when the place was filled with the older gents.

Gable spotted his target sitting in a large leather wing chair, alone by the wall.

Approaching in dread, and trying his damnedest to look confident, he cleared his throat, since the earl had not yet noticed him.

The gray-haired man was reviewing a stack of papers, his brow furrowed, when Gable interrupted. "Ahem. Lord Beresford," he forced out, "might I have a word with you, sir?"

"Ah, Roland." He put his papers aside. "Message from your father on the bill?"

"Er, no, sir. It concerns your daughter."

Beresford stared up at him, bemused. "Which one, Roland? I have six."

Gable swallowed hard. "Lady Katrina," he answered firmly.

"Oh?" Her father sat back and smiled, gesturing to the chair nearby. "Do sit, lad. Tell me, what's on your mind?"

CHAPTER 7

Eclipse

*T*hough Abigail's place at the table had been empty for a week now, their family dinners still felt strange. Trinny's chair was situated right across from the second-born's now empty one, leaving her to stare at the gaping hole in their family circle. Even though everyone was happy for their bride, they all secretly mourned her absence.

Life had changed forever in the Beresford household, but deep down, Trinny knew this was only the beginning.

Her younger siblings chatted about what exciting things the new Mrs. Freddie might be seeing on her way to Cornwall, where the newlyweds were taking their honeymoon. Of course, the two littlest ones were innocent as to the true purpose of a wedding trip.

All Trinny knew was that, with her sister's empty chair staring her in the face, there was no way to ignore her deepening terror of her own future. She glanced around at the table: two parents and the children. And in the years ahead, one by one, the rest of her sisters would also depart, off to start their own families…and she'd still be sitting here.

In the place of a child.

But no. She refused to regret her choice. She blocked such thoughts from her mind and forced herself to join the conversation cheerfully, confident that she'd get used to this.

After supper, all four of her sisters present got to work helping third-born Martha move out of the bedchamber she had shared with fourth-born Gwendolyn since toddlerhood. By order of precedence, Martha had been awarded Abigail's former room.

Betsy was still a little bitter about having lost out, since she often got her way through sheer willpower. But the youngest, Jane, was determined to be helpful. "Don't worry, Bets. If anyone ever *does* want to marry Trinny, you can have *her* room. Not that we're trying to get rid of you, Trin."

She laughed. "Of course not. I'm not going anywhere," she teased. Then the girls stampeded upstairs to get the move over with.

Even with the help of a couple servants, it was sure to be a tedious job, for Martha tended to be highly particular about how her things had to be arranged. She was a little obsessed with neatness and quite hated dust.

Trinny watched them all go clomping off, making no move to follow. Though it was the usual—or at least, self-appointed—task of the eldest to take charge and supervise such projects, she needed time alone. She was still too raw emotionally to join in the madness and inevitable chaos of the great move.

Instead, she made use of the last golden rays of sunset pouring into the drawing room to finally sit down and start working on her hats. Determined to create something of sufficient taste and gentility that would impress even the most fashionable milliners of London, she laid out all her supplies on the drawing room table.

She had purchased three plain bonnets and a variety of ribbons, beads, nice braiding, some lace and silk flowers, and even a little artificial bird that she was just dying to pin on the front of some hat, though she feared that might be her own eccentric taste tempting her a bit too far. *What woman really wants a bird on her head?* she wondered.

Nevertheless, merely taking out her wicker head form, her craft glue, and her almighty pincushion cheered her up considerably. *This is going to be fun,* she told herself.

But even still, she could not focus. Maybe it was just her sisters' elephantine footsteps and the bellows of normal family life coming from upstairs that made it difficult to concentrate. Plus, the artificial bird was staring at her with its beady little eyes. She turned it around, then tried again.

Right. Determined to keep her mind distracted with any topic that wasn't Gable, she started draping various types of ribbon around the first bonnet's crown, trying this and that without committing to anything yet.

After all, she had the entire night to decide.

And the night after that.

And the night after that…

She swallowed hard as another tremor of dread shook through her. For one terrified heartbeat, she stared unseeingly at the array of colorful fripperies before her, while the clock's tick-tock boomed in the relative quiet of the drawing room, and the long, empty evening stretched out before her.

Well, she'd better get used to it. Find a way to fill the time. Find a way not to die of loneliness. How was it even possible to miss someone you had only known for a few weeks?

She shoved Lord Sweet Cheeks out of her mind with a will, resolved to make him once again the stranger that he used to be to her. She even refused to acknowledge that it was the night of the lunar eclipse he'd mentioned. It had said so in the paper.

She refused to think of him setting his telescope up on his roof across the street, watching the moon disappear into blackness and then return again.

If he even remembered. If he wasn't already lost in dissipation this evening with his handsome rakehell friends…

Get out of my head, you bounder!

"Ahem." She shook off thoughts of him, took a deep breath, and then decided to pin the blue ribbon around the crown of the first bonnet. A boring choice, maybe, but that shade of cornflower blue would be flattering to nearly anyone, and besides, this was just the first step.

At least it was a start.

She had better come up with something brilliant soon, she mused, since she had staked her future on this. It was supposed to satisfy her for a long time to come, after all, and even earn her a little genteel income. But her heart kept asking, *Is this all there is?*

She suddenly jabbed her finger with a pin and let out a yelp of pain.

She dropped the hat—pins, ribbon, and all—and immediately looked at the red dot on her fingertip, her eyes smarting. And then, out of all proportion to the tiny wound, real tears filled her eyes. *Even the hats hate me.*

Oh, not again! she thought in annoyance. Good God, she had been a watering pot of late. She had managed to hide it from her family so far, refusing to let them hear her weep or see her mope, but at that moment, with her tears falling on her fripperies, Betsy and Jane came tromping into the room.

"I'm not helping her if all she's going to do is yell at me! How am I supposed to know what shelf Martha wants her stupid Wedgwood figurines to go on?"

"At least she wasn't giving you all the heaviest boxes—"

The bickering stopped abruptly.

The two youngest Glendon girls froze at the sight of their eldest sister bawling like a cake head over a bunch of hats.

They looked at each other in distress, and then gaped at her again.

"What's wrong?" Betsy demanded in her blunt way.

"What do you think?" Jane whispered at her in annoyance.

"I'm fine," Trinny sobbed out. "Please go away."

"No," her sisters said in unison.

Trinny cast about for something to dry her eyes with, but all she had was her sleeve. It was pointless, anyway. Now that she had started, she couldn't stop crying. It was dreadful.

She hated that her little sisters were seeing her like this. They were but children, and the eldest was supposed to be a pillar of strength.

They crept over uncertainly to her, one on either side.

"What's wrong?" Jane asked, laying a hand on Trinny's shoulder.

"You'd better tell us or we'll go and get Mama," Bets threatened.

"Don't…" They were too young to understand the subtleties of her foolish heart, no doubt, but Trinny was too burdened to hold back her grief anymore. She couldn't hold back. "It's just, I see it now—what I did wrong."

They sat down slowly on either side of her as the awful words escaped her in a whisper of blazing anguish.

"I'm not a quiz, I'm a coward. He was right."

"Who was right?" Betsy asked.

She didn't answer that, charging on in a strangled whisper. "I sabotaged myself at every turn. All my p-possible matches. I pushed them all away. And now here I am."

Jane tilted her head, gazing at her. "Didn't you like any of your suitors?"

"Some of them weren't so bad! And one," she choked out, "was wonderful. But I drove him away just like all the others. Because he's the one that scared me the most."

The girls stared at her somberly.

"What do you mean, scared you?" Bets asked, sneaking a glance around and keeping her voice down. "Did he try to, you know…take liberties?"

"No, nothing like that," Trinny said, shaking her head.

"Then what were you afraid of?" Jane persisted in concern.

"Honestly, I don't even know now. I-I guess I was afraid of getting hurt, because, deep down, I didn't really think I was good enough for him," she breathed, trembling. "That it was a fluke that he ever noticed me in the first place and his interest would soon pass. So rather than risk getting hurt, I pushed him away before he got a chance to reject *me*. And now look at me! I brought the thing I feared upon myself."

The girls gazed at her for a long moment.

"Well, you still have us, Trinny," Jane said softly. "We're your sisters, and we'll always love you."

Bets gave a solemn nod. "Even if you are an odd duck."

With that, both girls hugged her, and Trinny cried harder, but only for a bit.

At length, comforted by their sweetness, she managed to regain at least some of her composure. "Thank you," she said with a sniffle. "Would one of you dear things please fetch me a handkerchief?"

Headstrong Bets must have been sitting there longing to flee the drama, for she jumped up at once and dashed off to carry out this request without so much as a put-upon eye roll.

Jane patted Trinny's shoulder again, frowning with concern, waiting with her for Betsy to bring back the handkerchief. Once she did so, Trinny blew her nose and wiped away her tears.

Her sisters then endeavored to make her smile and had changed the subject to something inane when Papa happened to walk by the open doorway.

"Oh, there you are," he said, and came back.

As he walked in, the earl's watchful gaze skimmed his eldest daughter's face, probably noting the messy, telltale signs of recent tears—swollen eyes, red nose, and general beaten-up air—but he did not address it.

Nor did he look surprised.

She cleared her throat and tried to act natural. "Was there something you wanted, Papa?"

"Actually, a courier just delivered this for you." He came toward her carrying a small letter. "I think it's an invitation of some sort."

Before handing it to her, he bent down and gave her a kiss on her temple. "And my dear?" he whispered. "You have my permission to accept."

With that, Papa handed her the missive, tugged affectionately on a lock of Jane's hair, then walked out.

The youngest skipped out after him. "Papa, did you know Mrs. Faber's cat had kittens? They're *so cute!*"

"The answer is no, and you should be getting ready for bed," he said, but Jane persisted, pleading as only the baby of the family could plead, the two of them vanishing down the hallway.

"Who's it from?" Bets asked, nodding at the letter.

Trinny furrowed her brow. "It doesn't say. Lady Delphine asked me if I wanted to join her book club. I think it meets tomorrow. But I don't see why Papa would make a point of giving me permission to go to that…"

She cracked the seal and unfolded the little letter. The message was very short.

Meet me at the gazebo at ten tonight. We need to talk. Please.
Roland

Trinny gasped, jolted, and her fingers flew to her lips.

"Well?" Betsy demanded.

"Er, I was right. Just the book club," she forced out, barely able to speak.

Betsy narrowed her eyes. "Then why do you look like you're going to faint?"

"B-because she says we'll be reading Lord Byron."

"Ohhh. Maybe I'll tell Mama!"

"Elizabeth Anne!"

"Just teasing. Oh, Lord Byron, you're so wicked!" she mimicked as she flounced off making kissing noises and trying to taunt a reaction out of her eldest sister.

Trinny waited until the little menace had gone, holding the letter flat against her chest.

She did not need an overly curious fifteen-year-old nosing in when her world was suddenly spinning out of control. After all, maybe she had read it wrong. Maybe her eyes had deceived her from all her wishful thinking…

Hoping against hope, she peeled the letter back from her chest and warily peeked at it again, then gulped. What did he want to tell her? Was it good news or bad?

Did he want to reconcile or merely see the look on her face when he informed her that he'd pledged himself to another girl from his father's bride list?

The question shook her.

Still bewildered by her father's cryptic comment, her mind was in too much of a whirl to think clearly about it. She didn't trust herself in this state to figure it out until she heard the truth from Gable himself. She must not jump to conclusions. Her heart could not stand to be wrong on this point.

And she dared not be late. If she didn't appear on time, he might get angry all over again and leave.

Then she glanced at the clock and nearly shrieked to see that the appointed time for their rendezvous was only fifteen minutes away...and she still looked a wreck from crying.

She leaped up and flew out of the drawing room, leaving all her hats and supplies where they lay. She pounded up the stairs and pushed past the stream of her sisters and servants trudging back and forth between the two bedchambers with all of Martha's things.

"Excuse me!"

"You could help us!" Gwendolyn called in reproach.

"No time!" Rushing into her own chamber, Trinny shut the door behind her and seized upon the task of trying to make herself look presentable.

Crossing to the chest of drawers, she let out a yowl of horror when she saw her reflection in the mirror above it. She looked like a blubbering, red-nosed dud. And Gable was sure to be his usual calm, unflappably cool, and deliciously gorgeous self.

"Just perfect!" she hissed at her reflection as she poured water from the pitcher into the washbasin. Angrily splashing water on her face, she freshened her mouth, and, as an afterthought, changed out of her staid, spinsterish day gown into a pale muslin frock that was a little more lively and a bit lower cut.

She looked at the clock again and gulped, heart pounding.

She still had no idea what he was going to say, but she refused to look pathetic either way. She snatched her paisley shawl off the chairback on her way out of the room, then dashed down the upstairs hallway, went barreling down the steps, and only just remembered to grab the key to the park's gate off the hook outside the door.

Papa was sitting with his feet up, having a smoke in his study at the front of the house. She paused at the threshold and turned to her lifelong champion. "Did he say something to you, Papa?"

"I'll be here if you need me," was all he said, and sent her a wink.

Trinny shook her head, baffled, but there was no time to waste.

"Goodbye, my dear," her father said softly as she raced out of the house, pulling the door shut behind her.

Trinny hurried across the street, only then realizing her shoes didn't match her gown at all. *Blast it!* She'd forgotten to change them. But there was no time now. Oh well. He'd never notice. She fumbled with the key, squinting in the darkness, but finally unlocked the gate and stepped into the park.

She pulled it shut behind her with a bang, probably alerting him that she was on her way…if he hadn't already given up and left.

Then she ran to find him, unsure if she was bound for heaven or hell.

Running through the park like a wild thing made the neat chignon she'd worn in her hair all day start bouncing free of the combs meant to hold it in place, slipping sideways.

Lopsided hair, too! Oh, she was a prize.

Still, she didn't bother stopping, but pulled the combs out as she ran to him, shaking her long hair loose down her back, feeling gloriously free.

It did occur to her that when Gable saw her like this, out of breath and disheveled, her eyes still swollen from crying over him, he would know exactly how she felt. That she loved him desperately. That she saw now she couldn't be happy without him. That she was so sorry she had hurt him and insulted him, and that whatever his flaws, her life was empty without him. Even if he only wanted to be friends, she would accept that.

Anything…

Oh yes, one look at her like this and he'd know she'd come running when he called, but Trinny was past standing on her pride.

If he broke her into pieces tonight with the news that he'd found another future countess willing to accept his wicked ways just to get herself a castle and a man who would at least give her beautiful children, then so be it. In the midst of Trinny's cold terror, however, she clung to a small ray of hope. After all, Papa had seemed to know something…

The fanciful white gazebo came into sight, beguiling in the darkness. And there, pacing back and forth in front of it, was Gable, waiting for her.

When he turned sharply at the sound of her footsteps crunching on the graveled path, she slowed to a swift, nervous walk, her heart in her throat.

"I'm here!" she called out as loudly as she dared. She strode toward him, trying to look and sound more self-assured than she felt. "Sorry if I'm late."

"You're not late." He paused. Stared at her for a long moment. "I'd wait all night if need be," he said in a strange, ginger tone. "I'm just glad you came. Thank you."

They stood warily scrutinizing each other, and Trinny wasn't sure what to make of him. Gable was a man who masked his emotions as a matter of course. In the moonlight, it was all but impossible to read him. Still, she thought she detected a troubled look in his eyes. It was difficult to say.

A night bird cooed mournfully in the silence between them, and then they both started to speak at the same time.

"I wanted—"

"I wondered—"

They both stopped. Trinny cringed. *Awkward.*

Gable offered her a courteous nod, studying her as though he was trying just as hard to gauge *her* emotions as she was his.

"You wanted to see me?" she asked, then stood there waiting, with her nerves stretched as thin and taut as lyre strings.

For a long moment, he gazed at her, sadness creeping into his chiseled face, and this time, he let her see it. "You were right about me, Katrina. Your words, they cut me deeply," he uttered in a slow, soft tone. "But they also woke me up. I need you, you see. *You.* This has nothing to do with the money or the castle or anything of the sort. If I don't have you, I have nothing."

As he took a step closer, she looked up at him in wonder.

"I don't care anymore if my father cuts me off. I told him so. This has nothing to do with his wishes or any of the foolish things that mattered so much before I learned this unbearable lesson…of what it feels like to lose you."

She swallowed hard.

He shook his head, staring tenderly into her eyes. "Please come back to me, Katrina. All that matters now is having you by my side. Why I didn't see that from the start, I don't know. I've been…so incredibly foolish and immature and all the things you said I was—"

"No! I'm sorry for them all!" she whispered, laying her hand on his forearm as she drew closer. "I had no right to speak to you that way. You're a good person."

"Don't apologize, sweeting. On the contrary, I *owe* you for telling me the truth. I needed to hear it. And you were right." He shook his head and shrugged. "That's why I asked you here tonight. To let you know I'll do anything it takes to win you. I can't bear this anymore, being shut out of your life. I need you. I love you, Katrina, and I want to be with you and only you. Forever."

Her eyes widened in shock.

"Run away with me, tonight."

She drew in her breath. "Run away?" she echoed, feeling slightly dizzy.

"Let's elope to Gretna Green. I have my carriage waiting."

She took a step back, gaping at him in astonishment, clapping both her hands to her mouth.

"I know you've got your doubts about me," he said softly. "But I swear to you, if you'll give me another chance, you'll see that I've absolutely changed. *You* changed me.

"Believe me," he added, "I never anticipated this. I never would've thought it was possible for me. But I sincerely have no interest in that old life anymore. It's over. You're the only woman I desire. You must know I'm telling you the truth. I wouldn't lie to you. I never have," he said. "From that first night we met in this very spot, we've always been open and honest with each other, have we not?"

Hands still covering her mouth, her eyes as wide as saucers, she could only nod.

"So let me spend the years ahead figuring out every way I can devise to make you happy, darling. Will you marry me? Well? God, say something," he whispered.

Words were actually beyond her right then.

Instead, she let out a small, incoherent cry and launched herself into his arms.

He caught her around the waist and lifted her off her toes as she flung her arms around his neck.

"I love you, too!" she choked out at last.

"Thank God." As he held her close, burying his face against her neck, it was only then that she felt him trembling. "I was so sure I'd lost you." He squeezed her even tighter. "I love you. I never knew it could be like this."

"I love you, too, Gable." She covered his smooth-shaved cheek in tearful kisses until he turned his face and caught her lips with his own.

"My darling," he breathed. He set her on her feet and claimed her mouth in rapturous hunger.

Trinny clutched his lapels and pulled him down to her, desperate for more of his kisses. Just being with him again soothed her soul, and his declaration of love had her giddy.

He kissed her again and again, his warm, gentle hand sliding into the curve of her nape under the fall of her hair.

She tore away from his breathless kisses. "You really want to marry me?"

"Yes. I insist on it, actually. Didn't your father tell you I spoke to him today?"

"So that's what he meant," she whispered slowly, fresh tears filling her eyes.

Gable smiled fondly at her. "You didn't realize I summoned you out here to ask for your hand?"

"Why would I assume such a thing?" she exclaimed. "Nobody ever wants to marry me!"

"Oh, I do, sweeting." He took hold of her shoulders and looked fiercely into her eyes. "I am *so* glad none of those other fellows ever proposed to you. If you'd said yes to one of them, my whole life would've been ruined."

She held his gaze somberly. "Something in me must've known to wait for you. My true love."

"My darling girl," he murmured, visibly moved by her artless words. He gathered her into his embrace and held her like he'd never let her go.

Trinny rested her head on his chest, profound relief mingling with her joy and trembling gratitude as he cradled her head against his heart.

"Can we really leave tonight?" she whispered.

"Right now," he promised. "Shall we?"

They parted a small space, but he captured her hand, linking his fingers through hers.

"Elope with me?" he asked.

"Well…as long as you're sure," she said. "Because, you realize, if we do this, you're stuck with me."

A tender smile spread across his face. "That, my dear, sounds like my idea of paradise."

A teary-eyed laugh burst from her. "Then take me to your carriage!"

He lifted her hand and kissed it, and then he did just that.

As they walked away from the gazebo, Trinny's feet barely touched the ground. Gable led her through the moon-silvered park, down the winding path to the opposite side of the square, and out the other gate, where an elegant coach-and-four waited.

Hurrying by his side, Trinny did not look back, not to get her things or even to consult her parents. Papa would know when she didn't return that her answer had been yes, and then he'd tell her mother and the girls.

She'd write them a letter from Scotland once she was married, and she'd sign it *Lady Roland*.

Gable got the carriage door for her and, with a jubilant note in his deep voice, ordered his driver to head north. Then he handed her up into the coach, where a bottle of champagne waited on ice. It was a while before they opened it, however, many miles up the road. First they had more pressing matters to attend to.

Wrapped in each other's arms, they had to make up for lost time.

EPILOGUE

Queen of Castle McCray

Three weeks later

*I*n all her life, Trinny never thought she'd end up as the lady of a castle, married to a man as beautiful and good as Gable Winston-McCray, Viscount Roland.

Or Lord Sweet Cheeks, as she still preferred to call him. But she was Lady Sweet Cheeks now, and here she sat, on a bench on a chilly Scottish day in early June, watching the crashing waves of the North Sea, hoping to see another whale out there, all while cozily wrapped up in a red-and-blue wool tartan blanket of the clan McCray.

Her family now, too.

Overhead, the afternoon sky was moodily dramatic, with sunbeams breaking through the clouds. The salt wind tossed her red hair about her shoulders. Her husband had gone inside to fetch them hot drinks to keep them warm. Frankly, it was good to come up for air, as this was one of the few times they'd even left the bedroom. To be sure, being married to a reformed rakehell had its advantages.

A mischievous smile tugged at her lips as she pulled her feet up onto the bench and wrapped her arms around her bent knees, staring at the waves.

That wonderfully depraved lover of hers did things to her that took her to heaven and sent her home again in a box of candy. After three weeks of his almost nonstop lovemaking, she had become something of an expert herself already, not to brag.

And, oh, those sweet cheeks of his! Their lean, muscled curves were even more adorable bare, and it made her very jolly to give them a good little spanking every now and then, which the rogue protested but clearly enjoyed.

His cute male derriere, however, was just the beginning of her man's countless beauties. She was still as dazed by the breathtaking wonder of his muscular body as she had been the first time they had been naked together, on their wedding night.

Her deflowering had hurt a bit, though he had been gentle, but everything since had been sheer bliss. She felt so close to him since they'd become lovers, and his complete acceptance of her had set her free. Sometimes she was a little shocked at her own enthusiasm, but what could she do? Her wicked playmate drove her deliciously mad. Whether riding him in a frenzy in their huge canopy bed or being ravished by him on the kitchen table—or in any other random room of the castle that caught their fancy—she was desperately in love with him, and he with her. More deeply every day.

She gazed down again wistfully at the ring on her finger and smiled in lingering amazement. Thinking back to the heart-tugging ceremony at the famous blacksmith's forge at Gretna Green, she would not have had her wedding any other way.

"This should keep you warm!" he called just then from behind her.

She turned and saw him heading toward her—lord of the castle that loomed just a few hundred yards up the emerald slope. A smile spread across her face at the sight of her mate and best friend.

"Here comes my love," she greeted him cheerfully as he returned to join her in the mesmerizing ritual of watching the waves roll in and crash over the boulders below. The wind ran rampant through his glossy black hair as he carried two sturdy mugs in his hands. "What did you bring me, husband?"

"Hot chocolate."

"Angel!"

"Here." He handed her one of the steaming mugs, and she curled her fingers around it, warming her hands.

"Thank you." She kissed him for his pains.

Gable sat down beside her and joined her under the tartan blanket with a playful shiver. "I need my wife to keep me warm."

"That's what I'm here for." She cuddled against him under the blanket, feeling very cozy indeed.

"Mmm, that's better. Here, a letter came for you."

"Really?"

"It's from your mother." He took it out of his pocket and handed it to her.

"I'd almost forgotten the rest of the world exists," she said softly, glancing at him as she took the letter from him.

"We don't need it," he whispered, holding her gaze.

She tore herself out of his potent spell. Honestly, he could enchant her with one look, but thankfully, she managed to keep her wits about her.

"Well, let's see if there's any interesting news from home or any juicy new gossip from Moonlight Square..."

He curled his arm around her shoulders under the blanket and leaned his head against hers while she skimmed her mother's report on all the latest goings-on.

"Is your sister back in Town yet?" he mumbled.

"No..."

It seems so quiet around here with both you and Abigail gone. Martha's getting used to being the eldest in the house now, but all your sisters miss you terribly. Of course, that's nothing compared to your father's moping.

"Oh, Papa," Trinny said under her breath with a pang of affection. Gable glanced over inquiringly.

"He misses me and Abigail," she explained to her husband.

He smiled at her. "Can't blame him. But too bad, I'm keepin' you."

She grinned and read on.

Oh, I'm afraid I also have some sad news for you, dear. Old Lady Kirby died in her sleep two nights ago.

"Oh, no!" Trinny murmured in surprise.

They say she went peacefully, which is hardly how she lived, but I daresay you might want to write to your friend Miss Carvel and extend your sympathies at once. Her Ladyship's passing does not come as too great a shock, given her age, but I do hope the girl will be all right, orphaned as she is, and with her brother away on the far side of the world. The funeral is tomorrow...

"What is it?" Gable asked in concern.

When Trinny told him the sad news, he hugged her and pressed a comforting little kiss to her temple. "Well, I suppose she was very old, wasn't she?"

"Yes. She lived a good long life, full of adventure, from what I understand. Still… Poor Felicity."

"You want to go in and write her a note right now?"

Trinny nodded in regret. "If you don't mind."

"Come. You keep the blanket. I'll carry your drink for you."

He took her cup helpfully while she untangled herself from the tartan.

They got up from the bench and headed back across the green toward their castle. Its stones and towers glowed in a broad ray of sun, and they both gazed at it in wordless admiration as they walked. Meanwhile, the sough of the waves carried on with its endless, rhythmic song, churning at their backs. The lone cry of a gull hovering over the rocks seemed mournful, but Trinny couldn't help reflecting that endings, though sad, were as much a part of nature's great cycle as beginnings were.

At least now Lady Kirby had been reunited with her husband on the other side of the veil, she supposed. It made Trinny smile to think of the woman's free spirit, long trapped in a frail, elderly body, made young and beautiful again in whatever sort of intangible form people received when their souls left this earthly realm.

"So how much longer do you want to stay here, anyway?" Gable asked.

She smiled. "With you, I could stay here forever."

"My thoughts exactly."

"You're not getting restless to return to Town, then?" she asked.

"Not at all," he said. "I just wanted to make sure *you* weren't getting bored."

"No, you've been keeping me *very* entertained," she assured him with a gleam in her eye.

He grinned. "I aim to please."

"No hurry, then?" she pursued as they strolled home, side by side.

"No hurry at all," he answered gently, and when he sent her a reassuring sideways glance, she saw that love had turned his eyes the deep, soft blue of the sea.

Her heart clenched. *Oh, I love you.* She took her cup of cocoa back from him so she could hold his hand as they walked.

He got the door for her when they came to the threshold of his castle. "After you, my queen."

She accepted her husband's gallant gesture as her due but stole a kiss anyway as she brushed by.

"Oh, come back here, you. I want another one of those!" he said as she hurried inside.

"You'll have to catch me first!" She set her mug aside, dropped the blanket, and ran, laughter trailing behind her.

It wasn't long at all before he caught her...not far from their bedroom, conveniently.

They were already breathless with laughter and want as he swept her off her feet and carried her into their bedchamber.

As he claimed her mouth, tasting of sweet hot chocolate, their whole sad purpose for coming inside had been temporarily forgotten, but life was for the living, and Trinny had no doubt that Lady Kirby, of all people, would have understood—and categorically approved.

When you found the man you loved, you held on to him with all your heart and cherished every precious day fate granted you together. You took him in your arms and lived each moment to the fullest with unhesitating passion.

And so, Trinny reached over Gable's shoulder, pushed the bedroom door shut behind them, and did just that.

MOONLIGHT SQUARE, BOOK 1

Duke of Scandal

Romance is in the air at Moonlight Square ~ Regency London's most exclusive address!

Jason Hawthorne, the Duke of Netherford, made it clear to the young, lovesick Felicity Carvel long ago that nothing could ever happen between them. He has *earned* his reputation as the Duke of Scandal—and she's his best friend's little sister. For honor's sake, he vows to stay away from the lovely innocent. But six years of the wealthy libertine's life have left Jason empty and jaded, while Felicity has blossomed into a strong, beautiful woman, ripe for love and marriage.

When a sudden windfall makes her one of the most sought-after heiresses in London, chased all over Town by fortune-hunters, Jason knows he must keep the rogues at bay until her brother returns from his dangerous mission abroad. Unfortunately, the scandalous attraction between them has only grown to a searing intensity. Deep down, Felicity still wants Jason for her own. But after getting her heart broken once before by Naughty Netherford, does she dare attempt to play with fire again—and this time, can Jason resist?

Turn the Page for a Sneak Peek...

CHAPTER 1

The Accidental Heiress

"Are you sure this is really all right, dear?" Mrs. Brown asked with a fret as the ladies' town coach rolled along.

Miss Felicity Carvel pondered the question, but then could only sigh. *Honestly, I'm not sure of anything where that rogue is concerned.*

"Perhaps you should have sent another letter," her chaperone suggested.

"He's ignored the two I've already written," she answered with a shrug. Indeed, she suspected that her letters were, even now, sitting in a large basket of neglected correspondence on the duke's desk.

Naughty Netherford was too busy having fun.

Felicity shook her head. "If the matter were not so urgent, I should not have minded waiting, but under the circumstances… Well, don't worry, Mrs. Brown. We shan't be long," she assured the older lady. "And besides, we've taken every measure to ensure propriety." *As much as can be had when dealing with a rakehell of the first order.*

"Hmm, yes, well, I suppose it *is* early yet," her chaperone conceded. "With any luck, we may escape his neighbors' notice. These fashionable folk usually lie abed till noon. Keeping such late hours is not healthy," she added with a disapproving frown.

"No." Felicity leaned toward the carriage window, peering out at the aristocratic neighborhood into which their coach now turned. "This place certainly is impressive."

"You've been to Moonlight Square before."

"Only at night, for balls and such, actually. Never in the daytime."

"Ah," said Mrs. Brown.

At night, Moonlight Square had seemed to her to brood beneath the stars in elegant, lordly excess, like some dark, decadent poet…one of those dangerous Romantics.

Even now, the glistening spring morning full of sunshine and birdsong could not quite dispel the eerie cast of melancholy reflecting off all the smooth Portland stone facades. Perhaps its sinister history as a hanging ground explained the pall of gloom that still hung over the place despite its current terraced perfection, all classical, columned porticoes and lacy wrought iron balconies.

In antique maps of London the area was labeled Hell's Watch, but a decade ago, the Prince Regent's own architect, Mr. Beau Nash, had built the magnificent garden square right overtop of the old, macabre memories of public executions and doomed rogues hanging in man-cages.

Nowadays the *ton* called this place Olympus on account of all the peers who had moved in. With a duke on every blasted corner, it might as well have been the home of the gods. And yet it did seem to attract a certain type of resident...

The wild, dark lords of Moonlight Square definitely made up their own dangerous breed. They fit right in with the haunted atmosphere that still lingered in this place, as though they were drawn to it. Each an island of gloom and brooding isolation unto himself, they drifted through Society like great, ominous thunderheads, crackling with the tension of pent-up lightning and liable to rage into a storm at any moment.

No wonder *he* had moved here...

At that moment, Felicity's driver, Thomas, slowed the clip-clopping horses to a halt before the giant corner mansion of the Duke of Netherford.

Right on cue, she felt her foolish heart begin to pound. She leaned toward the window, letting her gaze travel slowly upward over the five-storied splendor of his London mansion. She shook her head to herself.

Lud, sometimes it was hard to believe that the scandalous seducer who dwelled in such pomp was the same wiry rascal of a boy who had gone traipsing through the countryside with her and her elder brother, Peter, growing up. Or rather, the boys had gone traipsing. She, four years younger and a mere *girl*—as though it were a disease—had been tolerated only so long as she could keep up.

What happened to us all? she wondered. *We used to be so close. We used to have such fun.*

Wistfulness filled her for the happy childhood that had faded like a dream. She had known such freedom then, and *he* had once been innocent.

But that was long ago.

Ah, well. It was obvious what had happened: they had all three grown up. Life had taken its toll on each of them in various distinct ways, and now here they were.

Of course, her brother and Jason were still as thick as thieves, but Felicity had long since been left out of the equation. Oh, she had brought it on herself through her own youthful folly, throwing herself at her brother's best friend that humiliating day eight years ago.

She closed her eyes with a faint wince at the memory.

Jason's gentle rebuff still hurt a bit to this day, truth be told. Thankfully, however, she was long over her painfully intense infatuation with the heir to the Netherford dukedom, who had grown up on the neighboring estate.

She supposed any girl might have fallen for him back then. He was funny and kind and took an interest in what she had to say; he was reliable and good-hearted, for all his teasing, merry roguery. It had been a concoction her young heart could not withstand. Unable to bear her secret adoration of him any longer, at the ripe old age of fifteen, she had finally confessed her devotion to the older boy.

The then nineteen-year-old Jason had been, in a word, horrified.

Felicity shook her head, cringing. Now twenty-three, she could not imagine what degree of everyday familiarity between them could have possibly made her imagine it was anything other than scandalous to plop herself down on his lap, drape her arms around his neck, and flirt with him the way she had, with a big, naïve, beaming smile.

He had gone quite ashen, and too late, she had realized he was aghast at the position in which she had put him. Instead of declaring his undying love in return, as she had somehow foolishly expected, he had set her aside, stood up stiffly, and walked out the door.

Later that evening, before she had even recovered from her shame, Peter had marched into her chamber and yelled at her for making a fool of herself, risking her reputation, and bothering his friend.

Things between her and Jason had never been the same after that.

She was lucky Peter had decided not to tell Mother, but he only kept it to himself because she was still fragile from losing Father the winter before to a fever. Peter, now the man of the house, had said it would probably "kill" their mother to hear that her daughter had behaved in such a fashion.

Ever since that day, Felicity had been very careful to comport herself with the utmost prim-and-proper rectitude at all times. No matter how bored she grew with her existence sometimes. No matter how much she might resent it.

Ah, but back then, in her tearful innocence, she had told her brother she had honestly thought her beloved Jason *liked* bold girls. Based on some rather scandalous conversations she'd overheard between the two rowdy young bucks, it was an understandable mistake. And she had *so* wanted Jason to love her as she loved him—for himself—who he was, not for his dukedom or his wealth or anything like that. Such things were meaningless to a lovesick girl of fifteen.

But alas, her moment of brash forwardness had ruined everything between them. Jason had all but forgotten she existed, particularly after he had ascended to the title, taking the place of his horrid cold fish of a father.

Felicity could only pray that perhaps by now he had forgotten the whole embarrassing debacle. Likely he had, given the sea of women who regularly threw themselves these days at the hard, polished libertine he'd become.

Still, that was no excuse for him to ignore both of her frantic letters. It wasn't as though she expected such an *important* personage as the Duke of Netherford to give her a personal response. She was quite content to deal with His Grace's secretary.

All she wanted was one simple piece of information: whether or not he was able to get a message to her brother for her.

It was urgent, and since Jason could apparently not be bothered to answer his mail, she had come in person to get the details she needed from someone, anyone, on the duke's staff.

As her coachman walked back from the driver's box to hand the ladies down and her footman ran her card up to the front door, Mrs. Brown tapped Felicity on the shoulder. "My dear?"

About to get out of the vehicle, she glanced back at the matron. "Yes, ma'am?"

"What will you do if we see the duke?" Mrs. Brown asked, worry in her dark eyes.

Words quite failed Felicity at the question.

Hope the earth opens up and swallows me?

About the Author

Noted for her "complex, subtly shaded characters, richly sensual love scenes, and elegantly fluid prose" (*Booklist*), Gaelen Foley is the *New York Times*, *USA Today*, and *Publisher's Weekly* bestselling author of twenty historical romances from Random House/Ballantine and HarperCollins. Her award-winning novels are available worldwide in seventeen languages, with millions of copies sold. Gaelen holds a BA in English Literature and lives in Pennsylvania with her husband, Eric, with whom she also co-writes family-friendly "PG-Rated" fantasy adventure novels for kids and adults under the penname E.G. Foley. (Book One in their Gryphon Chronicles series, *The Lost Heir*, has been optioned for a movie!)

Visit www.GaelenFoley.com and sign up for her mailing list if you'd like to receive an email alert when her next book is available. As a *Thank You* for signing up, you'll receive her famous *Regency Glossary*—a **free** 52-page booklet (PDF) chock full of fun little historical tidbits to enhance your Regency reading pleasure. Gaelen also holds occasional sweepstakes exclusively for subscribers, so there might be a prize in your future if you're one of her lucky winners.

Thanks for reading!